UNDERWORLD RISING

by

Manuel Ruiz[3]

DEDICATION

For my Grandparents.

Thank you for giving me and my brothers a second
home in Alice, Texas. I love and miss you dearly.

Paternal
Manuel "Buelo" Ruiz, Sr.
Eulalia "Buela Lala" Ruiz

Maternal
Ramiro "Bempa" Treviño
Ercilia "Memo" Treviño

I'll see you in my dreams.

CONTENTS

ACKNOWLEDGMENTS

Thanks to the following:

The incredible young readers and writers I have
been fortunate to have met at book events and
school visits over the last few years. You inspire
me more than you could ever know.

The librarians from my school days who always knew
just the right book to suggest for my next great read.

Molly Kusel – Wynn Seale Jr. High
Pam Allen – Robstown High School

My Daisy and Kristopher. Always.

Special thanks to Grey and The Dead Club
for letting me tell their story.

CHAPTER 1:
HOPE

My name is Grey Gomez. I'm the leader of The Dead Club, which was originally made up of five members that all died around the same time and were brought together to help stop an unknown force that broke the Underworld. We figured out that we all had abilities related to how we died and came together to defeat our enemies. However, that fight broke a hole in the Underworld that freed souls that were scattered throughout the lands due to punishment, banishment or hibernation. This included a race called the Forta, who were the original, cruel beings that once ruled the Underworld, and have now returned to reclaim their rule.

They have infiltrated the Underworld Council, imprisoned the Keepers of the Underworld and kidnapped my friend the Oracle, who led a rebellion to defeat them many years ago.

Then there's the current status of our core Dead Club. Brianna, an original member who left to the other side, seems to have returned although she is not all here and can only appear in short bursts.

We have also lost Andi. She was the first person I met when I arrived and has become my closest friend. She's sour, she's sweet and stands her ground even though she is the smallest of us.

I want to be like her.

Somehow two traitorous Council members might have turned her. She seems to be helping them and although it's difficult for me to believe she has betrayed us of her own free will, we simply don't know.

The only members of the Club left are Cal the baseball player, Blue the super scientist and me. Although not a full Dead Club member, we also have Leo the Librarian of the Underworld on our side.

We took a hard loss and are in tatters, but the four of us remaining aren't giving up. In fact, we are currently developing a plan here in the tech room of the library. We know we can't win this battle alone, but a communication network Blue built may have given us a real possibility at saving our friends. We need to gather as many allies as we can if we are to have any real chance of stopping the Forta. The Grim Reaper, who the Forta removed from the fight by threatening his girlfriend the Oracle, told me about a secret Leo had shared with him years ago to get into the supposedly impenetrable Council Chambers, where the traitor Councilmen and Andi are. I hope that this will be our first step to a master plan. Right now, we are outnumbered and have been outsmarted. Hope is all we have.

"Grey, are you talking to yourself?" Cal asked.

"I promised Kristopher I'd explain everything to him, so I've been keeping a personal audio log for a while. Figured I would remember more details hearing it than if I wrote it down. Leo suggested it."

Kristopher. My best friend who is still alive and back on Earth. I had found a way to communicate with him through his computer via the Underworld network Blue was building. I hoped to talk to him again soon.

"Yes," said Leo. "As Underworld Historian, I would encourage all of you to keep a personal log for future reference."

"You're assuming we'll all live through this," Cal said.

"As I must. As you all must. Let us return to our planning."

I nodded. Our brief break to gather ourselves was over and this log had helped me clear my thoughts.

"Leo, please tell us more about the plan Grim was talking about to break into the Council Chambers," I said.

He raised his hands and a batch of about fifty books appeared above us, flying in from the shelves in the main library.

"This many?"

"Yes, of course. Some of these books cannot be checked out without the permission of me and the Council and most of these are unlisted, so most creatures don't know they exist. Even so, there are some Underworld secrets that could hurt the Council or the Underworld and possibly even destroy them, much like how Craver and Conniver used their information. For larger scale instructions, there are references from one book to another, ciphers in others and the like that all have to be brought together to get the entire instructions on what to do. Some things are too dangerous to have in one place."

"Grim said you knew a way."

"Yes, from these books, I played a game many years ago to find out how to break into the Council Chambers and steal something precious. I must link the books now in my head to see."

"But you said you did that years ago?" Cal said. "Did you forget?"

"No, not at all, but it was just an idea at the time. The Grim One showed no interest, so I didn't take it any further all those centuries ago. It's possible some things have changed over time. I need to get the latest information available. If anything has changed, the books will have rewritten themselves."

The books glowed and their pages flipped, then pages flew out from each book and mixed with each other, glowing and dancing in the air. Finally, three empty covers appeared. The pages made a popping noise and started to duplicate. After a few moments, half the pages returned to their books and the other half jumped into the three empty covers, forming three separate books. They floated down on the table.

"These books contain temporary copies of the key pages for ease. They will cease to exist shortly after we get what we need. There are items here we need to visualize," Leo said.

One book opened and there was a picture of a tree.

"This tree will tell you how to reach the Council Chamber. It will be difficult to find, and this tree is unique in that it has a soul. It is connected to all the Underworld vegetation and collectively will speak to them and show you the way."

"You know I can already track the Council Headquarters, right?" Blue interrupted.

Leo opened his mouth. "I did not consider that. No one's been able to do so until now. I suppose we do not need this book."

That one disappeared, leaving the two.

"The next step after discovering how to get to the Council grounds is how to get in. The tree would normally appear on the outer grounds once it directed you on how to find it, but since that's not necessary, it's the next feature that is critical. This tree will reveal the location of a secret key."

"A secret key?" Cal asked. "Like leaving a spare in a fake rock in your bushes?"

Leo looked him up and down. "That's extremely crude but close. However, you would always know where the fake rock would be. In this case, the tree must reveal where the secret key is hidden. It should be outside the castle, but would not be easy to find and moves to different locations randomly. The sheer size of the chamber and the emptiness around it could take years to explore if you did not have this information."

"So then we need to get to the tree," I said. "How do we get there unnoticed, though?"

"That information is not in one of these books. There is no visual aid, but from my own knowledge I can tell you that there is an option."

"What about the coats the Forta used to hide themselves? Can't we use those?" Blue asked.

Leo shook his head. "No, the Oracle had them last and I have no idea where they are anymore. Even if I did, after the Council and the Oracle inspected them, they were no longer working."

"What else?" Cal asked.

"This will not be pleasant."

"What is it?" Blue asked.

"You will need to cover yourself with a specific animal's substance. This is something I discovered many years ago and is not common knowledge. I believe I may be the only one aware of this animal's special properties."

"How come only you know this?"

"As the Librarian, I know of all types of information on

Underworlders, even the most seemingly insignificant details. I also collect information on the unseen creatures that reside here. Some are small animals, but there is one specific species here that lives under the ground. They look like underground food, similar to small, thin potatoes, but they are living creatures. They move no more than an inch or two a day, are like a snail or worm on Earth, but they have something unique that is undocumented. I only found out by accident and I believe no Underworld creature knows anything about this except for me. I did share this with Grim, although he has since admitted he wasn't paying much attention so I can only assume this information has not been shared further."

"So what's the big deal about this animal?" Cal asked.

"They are undetectable, even by the strongest telepaths."

"How is that possible?" I asked.

"Their molecular structure is so slow that for one to detect them, they would have to use a much lower frequency. They would have to have the patience to try to detect them for several hours until they tried to move, but what reason would anyone have to do so? They pose no threat and as far as anyone is concerned, they serve no purpose. They do help keep our ground soft and smooth in certain areas. Otherwise, they simply live."

"So since you discovered them, did you get to name the species?" Blue asked.

"Yes, of course. *Ignoretur Slimus. Ignoretur* meaning 'undetectable' in Latin."

"That is so cool," Blue said. "What do you mean when you say you found out by accident?"

"I was working with the Oracle a long time ago when I was studying them. One of my questions was what their mental signature might look like. I am able to communicate with other Underworlders but not something like these creatures. I asked the Oracle to describe it for documentation, but she had trouble doing so at first. Eventually she caught something, but it took a long time. I wanted to know if other telepaths would have the same trouble connecting so I tried it with two others without telling them what I was looking for. They never sensed anything."

"I don't get it," Cal said. "So how do we use them?"

"You can wear their skin," Leo said. "It will be a little uncomfortable, but their scent would be virtually undetectable. If anyone was looking for you, they wouldn't notice the scent since it would just be like they were smelling or sensing the ground. No one is scanning for the material under our feet."

"That doesn't sound too bad," Blue said. "Will they have to die for us to take their skin?"

"No, not at all. However, you will need enough to cover each of you, and there is the slime factor."

"Slime factor?" Blue asked.

"Yes, their skin is attached by a thin layer of slime. It helps so that their insides can move slow and their skin can catch up later. Their skin can and will grow back. It's a process, but a quick one. Once you have that slime on you, we can use their skin to form one big skin pack."

"That sounds nice and disgusting," Cal said. "How many are we going to need?"

"We'll have to see. I'd say at least thirty to start with. Fortunately they're abundant and easy to find in most areas. We even have some right outside the library."

"So if we can get in undetected, we have to find this tree and get it to show us the way into the Chambers?"

"That is correct."

"How do we get the tree to tell us?"

"This is where it gets complicated. The reason this was a perfect crime is that the tree will interact with you. Between Grim and me, I figured we could make a connection. I actually spoke to that tree a few millennia ago for something book-related. I used its bark to make a special item in my personal collection."

"So you just need to come with us, right?" Blue said.

Leo shook his head.

"He's an Underworlder," I said. "They'd detect him as soon as he arrived, even with the skin, I'd imagine?"

"Even with the skin. I am the Keeper of Knowledge and am here to serve the Council. They have unobstructed access to everything and we speak often. That bond built over all these years is too recognizable. They'd know it was me instantly."

"The way my dog knew it was me coming home and not my little brother," Cal said.

"Exactly."

"Looks like it's just us," I said. "Blue, can you track Andi remotely or do you need to stay here?"

"I can detect her at certain points but have to manually adjust once the Council Chamber shifts. I'd have to be here."

"That may be a better course," Leo said. "The fewer the better."

"Can we use him to help with the tree?" I asked.

"Just let the tree know you're there and your purpose. If you surprise it, it will shut down and ban you from speaking to it for a hundred years."

I nodded. Needed to make a big mental note of that one.

"Then let's go get... Leo, what did you call them again?" Cal asked.

"*Ignoretur Slimus.*"

"That's too science class for me," Cal said. "Let's go get us some slimeskin."

CHAPTER 2:
THE PERFECT CRIME

We left the library and Leo provided us with some shovels and bags. We only had to dig about two feet deep before we saw them. Just like Leo described, they looked like tiny odd shaped potatoes but showed no life. I tried to sense them but got almost nothing. It was like something was there, but just a hint of it.

After a few minutes, we had only collected about five.

"Leo, I thought you said these were abundant?" I said.

"Not as many here as other places."

"I have an idea how we can do this faster, but can we go somewhere safe where there are more?"

Leo thought for a moment.

"Yes, there are a few places. Follow me."

We portaled out and landed in a familiar place. We were just outside the Grand Outdoor Arena where the Forta had attacked Cal inside the dancing blobs. There were no bright lights or music this time. It looked abandoned.

"I guess with the current situation no one is coming out here to listen to music," I said.

"It would appear not," Leo said. "Let us get to the task at hand."

"So what was your big idea?" Blue asked.

"First, let's dig in and see what we have to work with," I said.

We started digging again. This time the potato bugs appeared every few feet.

"This should work," I said. "Blue, can you hit the ground hard with some water balls?"

He formed a small ball and smacked it into the ground. "Like this?"

"Yeah, but can you guide it? Make a small stream underneath them and then pull it up from under the dirt?"

"Good idea."

He shook his fingers and then shot a continuous stream under the ground. After a long streak, he raised his palms and the potato bugs shot up. We picked them out of the streams that were hovering in the air. He widened it to grab more and we moved around the concert grounds. Within twenty minutes we had four bags full of them.

"That should be plenty," Leo said. "Let's get back to the library."

We portaled back and walked into one of the hundreds of rooms in the library. This particular room only had a table and some chairs.

"One of my reading rooms," Leo said.

We emptied the potato bugs on the ground.

"How do we skin 'em?" Cal asked.

"This will be much easier," Leo said.

He grabbed a bug and held it up.

"Both of you grab one and hold it to your face," he instructed.

Cal and I did as we were told. I put it up to my right cheek. I could feel it slowly moving around as the ooze inside it gave way to the pressure of my grip.

"You just have to squeeze it from behind. Use your entire palm and try to force it to explode onto your face. Don't crush the center or you'll kill them. Just a gentle squeeze. Try it."

I wrapped my palm around its oval shape and squeezed gently, like my Mom taught me to do when testing an avocado. Nothing happened, so I squeezed harder. Then I heard a pop and a splat and felt the skin hit my face. The slimy side was on the outer part and not directly on my skin, but I felt it as it dripped down my cheek. It did not feel good.

Cal and Blue groaned.

I looked at the bug and it was completely black. Its brownish skin was gone, but I already saw new skin forming in patches.

"Don't worry about them," Leo said. "They will regenerate that skin and be totally covered in under an hour or so."

"The slime's on the other side of this gunk on my face. Do I have to flip it over?"

"No, just give it a moment. That slime has one purpose in life. To stick to another being. It will adjust."

As soon as he said it I felt the piece on my face start to move. It flipped itself over and now I felt the slime rub directly on my cheek and tighten.

"Gross," Blue said.

"Now grab more," Leo said. "Continue until you're covered. Leave spaces around your eyes and mouth. It will stick to your skin and clothing. It can sense the skin underneath. Just make sure you can breathe and see. Once it all comes together, it will thin out and just feel like a thick lotion."

We continued and it didn't get much better. I was glad I was wearing jeans, so I didn't have to feel the slime on my legs or lower body. The face and the exposed part of my arms were bad enough, especially when it got in my ears. Once I was completely covered, the worst was still to come. I felt every inch of the slime stretch and adjust as it conformed to my body.

Cal gagged. "Nasty! This is so nasty."

Once I felt the last movement, I opened my eyes.

Blue's eyes were wide as he stared at us.

"That was amazing!" he said.

Cal gave him a long gaze.

"Scientifically, I mean. I'm sure it wasn't that great for you guys."

"Not the most favorite experience of my life," Cal said.

"You should both be good," Leo said. "This will be enough."

"How are we going to get to the Council Chambers without our car? I mean, they'd find it, right?"

"You are correct," Leo said. "I have something that will get you there. You can't portal directly into the chamber now that your invite has been rescinded."

"What is it?" Cal and I asked at the same time.

Leo left the room and returned a few minutes later. He had something in his hand.

"What's that?" I asked.

"It is the key to your transportation," Leo answered. "Follow me."

We walked outside the library and Leo pointed upwards. "You see the gargoyles?"

I looked back up at the multiple gargoyles that lined the building.

"Those gargoyles come to life?" Cal asked.

"No, those are all statues. However, they represent and were modeled after actual gargoyles. The real gargoyles live in various parts of the Underworld but like these statues, they mostly keep to themselves. Even so, some of them will come if I call them. At least I hope they will."

He held up a small, white object that looked like a garage door opener. He raised it and clicked something twice.

"This is how you call them?" Blue asked.

"Yes, they are not telepathic but are friends. They should arrive shortly."

"Could they help us fight?" Cal asked.

"No, they haven't been a part of the Underworld core for a long time. They used to help with communication with their long-range ability to talk with each other through their high-pitched squawkish language. They would in rare cases help us with travel. They don't have much use to the main Underworlders anymore since we can almost all use telepathic connections to communicate and portals to travel."

"You mean that wasn't always the case?" I asked.

"No, back when the Forta ruled, they banned open communication for beings they considered beneath them and the Gargoyles were heavily depended on. Now they mostly keep to themselves but enjoy traveling around so I will see them every so often. Some stop by to catch up or say hello, but I think they just want to admire their likenesses here at the library."

"Interesting," Blue said.

We heard a sound in the distance. It was a soft windy sound, something I hadn't heard in a long time. Even the bird thing I saw in the darkness of Tenebris when I saw Grim barely made a sound.

I looked up and saw the wide and powerful wingspan

of two gargoyles. They moved fast and their wings looked strong. They approached and landed. They appeared to be the same size as the gargoyles up on the library. Their statues must have been to scale. They were at least seven feet tall and intimidating.

Leo walked up to them.

"Koda! Pido! Thank you for coming," Leo said. "It has been too long, but I have always enjoyed your company during your unexpected visits."

They lowered their heads in acknowledgment.

"Are you aware of the danger the Underworld is in?" Leo asked.

The gargoyle on the left clicked its teeth. "Yes, we are aware and hope that there is a positive outcome in the end."

"These young boys here," Leo started, "are trying to help. They are part of The Dead Club that stopped Craver and Conniver not so long ago."

"Yes, we did hear of this as well," Koda said. "The tale of the unexpected heroes has quickly become a grand tale."

"It has. A new chronicle to add to our history, but that story may only be the first of many. You both remember what it was like when the Forta ruled?"

They nodded their heads.

"It appears they are back. I need to get two of the boys to the Council Chambers without a portal. Can you please take them?"

"Yes, but as you know, we do not know the way to the Council."

"I have a way," Blue said. "I'll provide the information as soon as I have it."

"We'll have to get ourselves in sync on the network again, I presume," I said.

"Yes, we will," Blue replied. "We'll keep it short. I'll

head in and let you know as soon as I track Andi."

Blue returned to the library and we waited outside. I tried to link to him immediately in case he shot a message out to me. Within a minute I heard him.

"Grey, I just started looking for the signal. Shouldn't be long if nothing's changed."

"Okay," I thought to him.

"There!" he yelled. "Send Leo in here. I'm not sure where this is."

Leo rushed in. A few moments later Blue's voice popped in my head.

"Leo says this is a place called Dalcetta. The gargoyles should know where it is."

"Koda, Leo says to take us near Dalcetta and you would know where that is."

The gargoyles crouched enough to let us climb on their backs.

"Grab by the neck," Koda said. "Hold tight."

I did. Her skin looked smooth at first but was thick and rough to the touch. It didn't give much to grab onto like the skin of a horse. I had to really squeeze it and rub my fingers into her hide.

The gargoyles shot into the Underworld air.

Even with no natural wind, there was a breeze in my face with each flap of the Koda's mighty wings. The view was incredible and way different than when I was mind traveling. I had always been a little afraid of heights but other than a quick twinge in my stomach when we took off, I felt none of the same feelings I had when I was brave enough to ride on a roller coaster with Kristopher or the one time I had been on a plane when my family went to Disney World.

As we left the library, most of the ground underneath us was dark. Nothing like a plane where every so often you'd see a burst of lights from a large city. It was like flying over nothing, but there were occasional items that stood out. A raised hill at first, but then I saw a large mountain set. We flew near our old friend Elvis and his luxury location. I had only visited once since our encounter while we were chasing down some escaped creatures a few weeks ago.

Then more blackness.

"The Council's moved," Leo said in our heads. "Go Southwest."

I updated Koda and she did as instructed. After a few minutes, Blue broke in again. "It's on a far end of the Underworld now. Just cruise for a bit until we get a closer location."

After about twenty minutes of enjoying the flight, Blue came back in my head. "Now, go straight north!"

Koda and Pido moved quickly, knowing they were racing against the clock. We were overcome with cloud-like formations. They were orange and like dense smoke without a smell.

"Have them go east now," Blue said. "You should see something soon."

I instructed Koda and we shifted our path. I looked down but didn't see anything.

"Nothing," I thought back to Blue. "I don't see any kind of lights or anything."

"Hold on." Blue paused for a few seconds.

"Leo says part of the Underworld's protection is that you wouldn't see it unless you were much closer. I'll have to guide you."

Blue fed me instructions for a few moments to adjust the path and then broke in.

"Go straight down from where you are. The gargoyles are going to have to... wait, what?"

He stopped thinking into my head.

"What is it?" I asked.

"Leo says the gargoyles will have to drop you."

"You're kidding me, right?"

I thought of the time when I first met Blue and Cal. They were throwing themselves off a second-story balcony and survived. We were significantly higher than that.

"Leo says to assure you that you'll be okay. You'll just need a minute or so to heal."

"What about our slimeskin?"

"That will stay intact. That gooey stuff is pretty strong, according to Leo."

I let Koda know and looked over at Cal, who was updating Pido. I yelled across. "Ready?"

"Like this?" Cal screamed. "Do we have any parachutes?"

I shook my head. "Leo says we'll be fine."

"Now!" Blue yelled.

Cal stood on his legs and looked down. "No way. This is bull—"

The gargoyles flipped over, and we were free falling.

The air shot up slightly, giving some resistance. The feeling from my living days returned. My stomach was halfway up my throat and for a moment I couldn't think straight. We were falling into blackness and I couldn't see the ground.

"Leo says not to worry and to just enjoy the ride!" Blue yelled into our heads.

I looked up and saw Cal's arms flailing. His eyes were closed and he was screaming. I couldn't make out what he was yelling, but I could guess he was screaming what I felt.

I felt myself straighten and I was falling on my stomach with my arms and legs out. Cal was still flipping around. I took in a deep breath and tightened my fists. Then I saw shades of color as I fell closer. I saw different areas below me, some bright green colored ground to my left and a few small mountains to the right.

It was exhilarating.

I forgot my mission and the dire situation we were in for a few moments. The view was incredible, even without city lights. A few seconds later I saw it. The top of the floating Council Chamber. Different angle, but this was definitely it. We were falling several hundred yards from the building itself. Then it came fast. Within the next second, I went from a vague overhead view to the building being right there. I saw ground and then a small cluster of green that I was falling straight towards.

My face and body felt like they exploded as I landed on something that stabbed my side. I bounced and then landed on my back on the ground. I blacked out.

When I came to, I looked up and saw darkness. I felt more stabs of pain all over my body. It wasn't excruciating, but it didn't feel great. It was like I had way too much spicy chili and every part of my insides wanted to explode out. Then it got easier. The pain subsided. I reached up and felt my face. My skull felt like it was flat, but was expanding with each second.

CHAPTER 3:
UNINVITED

I heard a few cracks and pops, then felt okay to get up. I turned and saw Cal rubbing his head.

"That was a hard fall," he said.

"Are you okay?" Blue asked.

"Yes, we landed. Wasn't graceful, but we're here. How close are we to the tree?"

"You landed in an almost perfect spot. You should be in an area with vegetation."

"Yes, there's grass and bushes around us."

"Head toward the center of it. Just a little to your east."

I pointed right and Cal and I moved. It didn't take long. There was only one tall tree that had a full, round cap of leaves. We moved closer and saw it was about three stories tall. The bark was a dark reddish hue with specks of blue. As we got closer, I saw the specks were smaller leaves scattered around it.

Cal and I moved closer.

"So what do we do?" I asked.

"Leo said to lay your hands on the bark to let it know

you're there."

I moved up to the thick trunk. If Cal and I joined hands, we still wouldn't be able to wrap ourselves around it.

I placed my hands on the part of the tree in front of me and nodded towards Cal to do the same.

We both stood there for a minute and then I felt the tree move.

A soft red glow formed around our hands and grew. It formed an oval and started pulsing. A deep voice filled my head.

"You wish to enter the Council Chambers?" it asked.

I looked at Cal and saw him nodding. He could hear it, too.

"Yes," I said aloud.

"What are your intentions?" the voice asked.

I thought for a second. "To save our friends and the Council. To save the Underworld."

"And the other?"

Cal stammered and then took in a breath. "The same."

"Your true intentions must match your words to me. I shall verify your worthiness."

A thin branch popped out of the main trunk and stretched. Another one appeared. One was heading toward my face and another toward Cal's.

"What are you going to do?" I asked.

"I must probe you."

"Probe?" Cal asked. "Probe how, exactly?"

"I must feel your essence and examine your soul. Your true intentions will be revealed."

The piece of bark felt around my face. It was rough but didn't pierce the skin. It found the inside of my left nostril and started to move around.

"Are you going up my nose?" I asked.

"Seriously? Up our noses?" Cal said.

"I must enter somehow. There are other entrances on your bodies."

Cal and I looked at each other.

"Nose works," I said quickly.

The bark felt around just inside my nostril and then eased its way up. I could feel every part of it as it slowly moved up my nose and into my sinus cavity. I felt it inside my forehead. It wasn't painful but felt like I was being scratched on the inside by a bony finger. Then I felt a sharp pain as the bark popped into my head. It was inside my brain. Cal and I both yelled, more out of surprise than pain.

My fingers started shaking as the end of the bark moved around in my head. I had my eyes closed and tried not to think of what was happening. I once had a doctor stick a camera up my nose and thought it was the worst thing I had ever felt. I was wrong.

My head shook and I twisted with each probe and scratch from the bark in my head. Just when I thought I was going to jump away, the bark came back down and out.

I opened my eyes and scratched at my nose. Cal was holding his head.

"One of you did not tell me everything," the tree boomed.

"What are you talking about?" I asked.

"You," it said, its red orb moving in front of Cal. "State your full intention!"

Cal looked down. "I want to see if my friend Brianna is really here. I want to save her if she is. She saved me recently. I want to save the Underworld, too, though. This is just part of it."

The red circle pulsed a few more seconds.

"Your intentions are true," the tree finally said. "I am also part of this world. I may not be affected by whatever changes may happen, but I am aware that there is a dark

purpose emanating from the Council Chambers. I have no way of interfering, but will grant you access."

I sighed in relief. "How do we get in?" I asked.

I felt a flash inside my eyes and had to close them.

"You will be able to find the secret entrance in the rear of the chamber. I have given you both a one-time ability to view it."

I nodded. "Thank you."

"There is no need for gratitude. Your purpose and your souls are pure."

Cal and I left and headed out of the area and moved toward the Council. We both recognized the main entrance as we approached and took a long walk around to get to the back.

"Do you think they can detect us?" Cal whispered.

"Leo doesn't think so. Not sure if anyone's even listening or looking."

We went to the rear of the chamber and saw no obvious entry point along the long wall. We kept walking.

"Do you see anything?" I asked.

Cal shook his head.

"Maybe we're too far away," Cal said.

Made some sense. We moved slowly toward the wall. I was still worried something might see us so we kept low and moved slow.

Then I saw something.

A small light towards the left center of the chambers appeared. Cal pointed to it.

We moved a little faster and as we neared it, the light looked bigger. It wasn't exceptionally bright but definitely stood out. We reached it and as we got within a few feet, we saw that it was a single brick of whatever material was used to put the building together. I felt it. Smooth as glass, about a foot wide, and a little taller than a normal brick but still in a rectangular shape.

Cal tried to press on it, but nothing happened. I ran my fingers around the material that surrounded it.

"Blue," I called out in my head. "We are here and see the entrance, but can't do anything."

"Leo says he can't help you. You have to figure it out. He's never had to do this before."

I saw that this individual glass-like brick was surrounded by a thin adhesive of some kind. Like mortar. I ran my pinky finger around it. Nothing. Cal tried knocking. I thought about the tree for a moment.

"The tree gave us both access. Maybe we need to try it at the same time," I said.

I put my hand on the brick and Cal followed. As soon as he touched it, the brick's light dulled and disappeared. There was a small latch on it. I reached in and pulled. Didn't budge. Cal reached in, too, and this time it gave. I heard a scraping sound. A group of bricks pulled back in front of us and formed a square about four feet high. The bricks continued to shift back until they were gone and left a small doorway.

We crouched down and eased in. As soon as we walked in a few feet, the opening behind us closed.

"We're in," I said.

No response from Blue. Now that we were inside the chamber, our connection must have been broken.

There was no other direction for us to go, so we moved forward. We came out in an empty room, one I didn't recognize. It had a doorway and we opened it quietly and looked in. There was a hallway we started to move through and then I heard something.

It was a loud buzzing sound. We moved more cautiously and the buzzing grew as we moved.

We saw another set of doors. The buzzing was loud.

The doors had small holes in the center like a glass peephole. I was scared to look into one, but curiosity got the best of me. I slowly eased my eye in front of the hole and saw another eye looking right back at me. I jumped as it blinked.

"You are Dead Club?" a voice buzzed. The eye moved back and I saw what it was. It was a Keeper. It wasn't Bob. As similar as they looked, the voice was different. He was speaking aloud instead of in my head.

"Why you here?" it asked.

"We're trying to find our friends and stop this somehow. Is Bob back here, too?"

"Yes, two down."

I moved down two doors and looked inside. Bob the Keeper was there.

"Are you okay?" I asked him softly.

"Yes, all Keepers imprisoned. Separated us."

"Any way out of there?" Cal asked.

"Not from inside," he replied. "Open door."

"How? I don't even see a keyhole," Cal said.

"No key. Mental lock."

"The Councilmen must have a way to use their telepathy to lock these," I said.

"Can you undo it?" Cal asked.

"I'm not sure. If I try to scan this, they might detect us."

"Hey, we still got our slimeskin camo."

I nodded. It was worth a try. I put my hands on the door and then eased my mind like I wanted to scan it. I felt the power on the outer side. I could almost sense a vibration. It wasn't as intense as what I'd experienced during my travel through the Underworld atmosphere, but it was there. Like the door itself was vibrating. I tried to lock on, but I only sensed the crevices between each vibration.

"Bob, how much space would you need to get out?"

"Just small hole. Size of your finger."

I concentrated again. There was no way I was going to be able to open the entire thing. I thought smaller. The tip of a finger, just pressing against it, but it was solid. I shifted the sensation to the peephole. The outer line that was vibrating was much thinner. I pressed and felt it start to give, but it wasn't enough.

"What's wrong?" Cal asked.

"The peephole seems to be the weakest point. I can press it in a little, but can't push it through the door."

"Can I help?"

I thought for a moment. "Maybe you can help me push it through with that arm cannon."

"I got you," Cal said

He stepped back. I moved back a few steps to give him some room.

"Tell me when you're ready," Cal said.

I raised a hand to help me concentrate and felt the door vibrate again. I focused just on the peephole and nothing else. I pushed harder. I felt it start to press in, but it stopped moving. I turned my head towards Cal and nodded once, maintaining my mental grip.

Cal picked up his left arm and then straightened his fingers so his hand was flat. He popped out his arm, stared at the door and then went into a pitcher's windup. He whipped his arm and it almost whistled as it spun toward the door. The tip of his middle finger landed squarely on the peephole and I pushed as hard as I could as it struck. The clear glass broke through.

I let out a breath as I let my grip go.

Bob broke into his smaller pieces and a thin stream of his swarm pulled through. He reformed outside the door.

"Free Keepers," he said.

"No, that may be too soon. We need to find Andi and

see if our friend Brianna is here, too. We need to find some way to stop Councilmen Pink and Green."

"Will help search. Think I know where."

"Can you get us to them without us being noticed?" I asked.

"Yes. Follow me."

Bob the Keeper moved ahead of us. We continued down the hallway and then turned a quick left and then right. A stairway was there, almost completely hidden. You would have to have known it was there or accidentally ran into them to find it.

The Keeper moved up and we followed. We went up the winding stairway and it felt like we had gone up at least 3 or 4 flights when he turned into another room. We walked in and there was another hallway. We cut into the next opening and we were on an extended balcony that ran along a larger room. The Keeper's buzz quieted.

"They are here," he said softly.

"Who?" asked Cal.

"Rogue Council."

I eased up. There were railings on this balcony but they were solid. We'd have to stick our heads up and risk being seen.

I took my time to raise my head until my eyes were just over the railing.

The room below us was about the size of the Oracle's main ballroom. Councilmen Pink and Green were seated at a table to the left side of the room. They were in deep conversation.

"Andromeda!" Green yelled.

He returned to his conversation and pointed at the table where several pieces of paper and a few open books were thrown around them.

Then I saw her. It was Andi. She walked in and stood

there.

"Get us additional parchment and some drinks," Green said. "And hurry. I grow impatient with you."

Andi looked right at him and turned around. The conversation continued, but I couldn't make out everything. Something about a "first strike" and "dealing with the others."

Cal was also looking.

Andi returned a few minutes later with two goblets and a bunch of paper like those on the table. The council members took the parchment from under her arm and she placed their drinks in front of them.

"Andromeda," Green said. "Your friends. Do you think they'd be stupid enough to try and stop us?"

Andi stared back. "Yes, they will try. But they won't win. Not without Oracle or Grim."

"Your advice on the Grim One's weakness was correct. We are indebted to you."

Andi sat next to them.

I took a moment to soak in what I'd seen. Cal ducked his head and shook it.

The Dead Club had a traitor.

CHAPTER 4:
INFORMATION HEIST

We headed back down the steps and about halfway down Cal turned to me.

"There was no point trying to save her," he said through gritted teeth. "She turned on us."

I took a minute to think. As my shock subsided, I realized Andi would never turn so easily.

"I'm not so sure, Cal," I said.

"You heard and saw what I did, didn't you? She told them to take out the Oracle to keep Grim out! It was her idea!"

"We don't know everything. And we still need to stop them. We're here. What else can we do?"

"I don't know," Cal said.

"Bob," I said. "Do you think we have a chance at doing anything here?"

"Information," he said. "Plans. Possible advantage."

"We need a distraction," Cal said. "Like setting them up with a fastball just to take them out with a slow breaker right down the middle."

"We don't know this place well enough. And I didn't see any Forta."

"They have the Oracle, though, don't they?" Cal asked.

"Yes, but we don't know how many Forta there are. Some could be here, too. Look, we need those plans. Let's look around for something that might help us."

The Keeper buzzed below us. "I will."

"What?" I asked.

"Create distraction. I serve Council. With Council compromised, Keeper duty is to protect Underworld. Do not know if other Keepers will agree, but I know truth. Do not know where good Council is."

"When Cal and I were here last, I saw what happened," I said. "Councilman Pink used something called a dark portal to zap them away."

"Will check entire chamber."

"I'm pretty sure they're not here," I said. "We need to forget about the good Council right now. We need to get a hold of the documents they had on that table."

"But if we steal them, won't they just change their plans anyway?" Cal asked.

"Good point, but I may have something."

I talked it out quickly with Cal and Bob. It wasn't much, but we all agreed.

Bob took off and Cal and I ran back up the stairs to the balcony floor. We peeked over the railing and waited.

The Keeper flew into the room and created a mess with the papers. The council members jumped out of their seats and rushed toward Bob. He quickly zoomed out of the room. Andi followed them out.

I nodded to Cal and we leapt down onto the floor. I had no fear of this jump after falling from the Underworld sky earlier.

We rushed around the room. I gathered all the papers I

could and sat down as Cal tried to grab more.

I stared at the first of the few pages I had in my hands and took a mental note. I closed my eyes and tried to connect to Blue's network. It was closed to me, but I could still sense it. I isolated a pocket of energy, then quickly opened my eyes and stared at the page for several seconds. I repeated this until my hands were empty. Cal rushed to me with a stack of more papers, and then Andi came running in.

"What are you two doing?" she asked.

She wasn't angry or emotional.

"What do you care, traitor?" Cal said coldly.

Andi just stared at him but didn't say much else. "Those are not yours. Put them back!"

"Andi," I said, looking right into her face. "Andi, why are you helping them?"

"It is best for the Underworld that they rule. This is what must be done."

Her eyes were dull. Something was off.

"Andromeda!" Councilman Green screamed from another room. "Get over here!"

She looked at us both and then turned and ran.

"Drop everything!" I said.

"But we still have all of these!"

I dropped my stack and threw them across the room so they'd be in another mess. Cal hesitated a moment.

"We can't get caught, Cal. Let's go!"

He threw his papers in the opposite direction and we ran out of the room. The commotion was to our right. Bob did exactly what he was supposed to do. We ran back the other direction and made it back to the room where we had entered the first time.

Cal grabbed me.

"They're probably still distracted. Let's see if we can find the Council!"

"No," I said, sticking to the plan. "We need to go before they realize we were here."

"You don't think that little traitor is going to sell us out if she hasn't already? She's not one of us anymore!"

I shook my head and Cal's head snapped to the side. "Hey, what was that for?"

"What are you talking about?"

"You just mind-slapped me!"

It took me a second to realize what he said. "No, I didn't..."

And then I saw her. A familiar face, usually adorning a tiara, was behind Cal's shoulder.

"Cal, how could you think that?" her voice said gently.

He turned to see Brianna Angel's face staring back at him. She wasn't completely solid. She looked ghostly, but not pale or like she had on a cheap Halloween costume.

"Brianna, it's really you?" he gasped.

"Yes, and you're still a jerk! To think I saved you!"

"It was you! I knew it!"

She started to fade.

"Don't go!" Cal said.

"I can't control it," she said. "I'm only able to appear in bursts and I can't fully form. I've been here watching Andi. You have to know that isn't her."

"Sure looked and sounded like her. She betrayed us all," Cal said.

"No, not by her own will. They're controlling her somehow," Brianna said.

"That's what I'm trying to tell you, Cal," I said. "If anyone. I mean ANYONE, even Grim, were to talk to Andi the way Councilman Green did, what would she do?"

"You mean before or after she punched them in the face?" he asked, realizing what we were trying to tell him.

"She would have to be under the control or influence of something else. Our Andi would never put up with that. Not without a fight."

"Yes," Brianna said. "She is not herself."

She faded in and out again.

"Bri," I said. "What can you tell us about the council members and the Forta?"

"They are planning to take everything over, but they know they must defeat Grim and the Oracle before they can do it. They want to make the Oracle their slave, destroy her life and have her serve as an example to anyone who will ever think to oppose them."

"Do you know any details?"

"No, I haven't seen any Forta here. I've only heard the Councilmen talk about them, but I'm not able to stay long enough or get close enough to get enough details."

"How did you end up like this, Bri?" Cal asked.

"I was summoned. I was as happy as I could ever be with my Nana on the other side, but something kept telling me you all needed help. I wasn't sure how to get back exactly since it's usually forbidden, but I found a way. I tried breaking through a few times but something on this side was preventing me from coming through. I found enough strength to get in partially, but whatever is trying to take over is keeping me from getting here. The first time I appeared was when I knew you were in trouble in that glowy concert looking place. I thought you were gone, Cal."

"Thank you for that, by the way. I would have been if you hadn't shown up."

"You need to find a way to stop them. You don't have much time. Whatever they are planning, it's going to be soon. Within days."

She started to fade more. "I can't hold my form much

longer. It takes time for me to gather enough energy to appear.

"Then go recharge," I said. "Hopefully we can figure something out. Right now we have to go."

"We'll be back for you, Bri," Cal said. "That's a promise."

"Only if you also promise to come back for Andi, too."

"I assure you, we will," I said. "We're still a team and we will do whatever we can. We just have to be smart about it."

She nodded as she faded away.

"Let's go," I told Cal.

We ran back through the secret entrance and although the bricks were all reformed, we could still see a brick glowing slightly. It opened as soon as Cal and I touched it. We got out and ran back towards the tree.

The tree was dormant and I waited until we had reached it before trying to contact Blue.

"Blue, we're out. We have some information, but I need to figure out if I can send it to you."

"What do you mean?" he replied.

"We didn't want to let them know we were there, but I saw pages of their plan. I couldn't get a signal in there, so I stored it in my head, but I sent it up in the network as soon as we made it out."

"Whoah, cool," he said. "Glad you're both okay. Go ahead and try to send it."

I concentrated again and hoped my gamble had paid off. I had become in tune with the network but this was new. I sent images of what I could see up in the network cloud, but wasn't sure if I could retrieve them.

I was able to find my signal. I sent them straight out to Blue in the library computer source.

"Did you get them?" I asked.

"Something came through, but I can't read them."

"We can figure it out when we get back. Wait. How are we getting back?"

"Not sure, but Leo said it was covered."

He paused. "Leo said to wake up the tree and tell it you need passage out."

"How does that work?"

"Leo said to trust him. And not to panic."

"What is that supposed to mean?"

I didn't know how much time we had so I had Cal put his hands on the trunk again with me. The Tree's red oval came to life again.

"Returning so soon? I have already given you the ability to find the key."

"Yes, and thank you," I said. "We got in fine, although some instructions would have been helpful, for future reference. We need to leave. Leo the Librarian said you could give us passage."

"Yes, that I am able to do."

"How exactly are you going to get us out of here?" Cal asked.

"I am a tree first. My roots are deep and connect to other vegetation that is near the borders of this wandering plane of the Council Chambers. I can connect to the nearest vegetation and send you there."

"How exactly does that get us through?"

The red orb grew in size until it expanded to the bottom of the bark.

"Enter. This may be unpleasant."

"Worse than poking our brains through our noses?"

"It will be a different unpleasantness, but you will become one with the roots of our plane's vegetation. It is quite an honor as not many know this experience."

"An unpleasant honor. I guess honor us, then," Cal said.

"Enter."

I stuck my foot and then my leg in slowly. It tickled, but I felt my leg start to shrivel and distort. I looked at Cal.

"Ready?"

Cal nodded. "Just when you think we've seen the strangest stuff we'll ever see. Let's go!"

He dove in and I followed. I gasped as I felt my body squeeze and my bones crack. I was transforming. I moved down and as I turned, I saw Cal. He was in the shape of a human piece of licorice with smaller branches sticking out of him like a tree. His body color changed into a full red hue. I felt my body doing the same. My throat was squeezed so thin I thought I was going to implode, but my body adjusted and next thing I knew I was being sucked through tubes. It had to be the roots. I only saw flashes now but I could feel myself moving. I then felt my head start to expand again and my body felt like it was being blown up like a balloon of flesh. I heaved and a moment later I was lying on the ground. Cal was next to me. I saw his arms and legs make one final expansion and he looked normal again.

"That was not cool, but cool at the same time," Cal said.

"Yeah, I could go my entire dead life never doing that again."

We looked around. We were surrounded by some trees that were about ten feet tall with a thick layer of grass underneath us, but otherwise, there wasn't much.

"The tree got us out of there," I said to Blue. "What now?"

Before he could answer I heard a familiar swooshing sound. The gargoyles were back.

"The gargoyles should be there now that you're out of the Council Chamber's plane," Blue said.

"Yeah, a little late, but thanks."

I could sense the strength of our signal now that we were outside the zone.

The gargoyles lifted us up. We took another exhilarating ride and were soon back on the library grounds.

I dismounted and faced our new gargoyle friends. "Koda, Pido, we couldn't have done this without you. Thank you."

They both bowed.

"We wish you success, for the sake of all the Underworld," Koda said before they flew off.

They were grand creatures. I'd never look at the gargoyle statues the same again.

I ran into the library and yelled, "Blue, were you able to get the docs?"

He was banging on his keyboard. "I got them but I can't read them."

"What's the problem?"

"They are there, but these Underworld computers don't have basic programs I'd have on my regular machine at home."

"What do you mean?"

"I just need to convert these to a standard document or picture file or something similar. It is in a computer format now but I don't even have simple converter software."

"How hard is it to find one?"

"It's standard software for the most part on a machine, just not part of the Underworld hardware. I need a little more time to figure out how to get it."

I had an idea.

CHAPTER 5:
INVESTIGATION

"What about Kristopher?"

"What about him?" Blue asked.

"I was able to get my consciousness to him. Can I send him the documents on the same channel?"

Blue thought for a moment.

"You can get there without the Oracle?"

"I think so. I've been up in that Underworld cloud enough times and I've felt the sense of that power surge from when I made that first trip. Even without the Oracle's boost."

"If you can get there, I think I can keep the signal with you. Let me hook something up to you, first."

"Can we get rid of this gunk first?" Cal said, poking at the slimeskin that still covered our bodies.

With everything we had been through I had almost forgotten about it.

"Fortunately, removing them is much easier," Leo said.

He pulled out a device that looked like a hand vacuum cleaner. It was solid silver with a button centered near the top and small dime-sized holes on the end of it.

Leo walked up to Cal and placed the tip of the object on his chest. "This won't hurt, but it's going to make a loud noise."

He pressed the button and a crackle of what looked like lightning swarmed around Cal's body. The skin eased off him within seconds, falling to the ground in a puddle of ooze.

Leo pulled a container about the size of a coffee can out from under one of the tables. He got between the mess the skin had left and the container then zapped the ooze. This time he held on to the button and the electrical charge held on to the expelled skin. He raised it and the ooze rose with his movement and then he put it in a container.

Leo walked up to me and paused. "Ready?"

I nodded and he repeated the same process with me. I felt better but really needed a shower. Bug slime and becoming one with the roots and dirt of a tree are about as messy as I can take in one day.

I sat down on a chair as Blue handed me what looked like curved sunglasses.

"Put these on," he said.

I placed them over my face and ears.

"No, they go on your head."

He reached over and adjusted them. They looked like the hairbands my Mom wore over her head when she was going to be outside.

"What is this?"

"It's to help get the files there without corrupting them. Not sure how they'd carry with just your connection. Hopefully I'll be able to monitor the signal you carry and send my connection up with it."

"Can't I just send him the original files I saw?"

"No, I had to reverse engineer them here. They are in a

common format that I just can't convert. He should be able to do it. Just tell him to try to save them as any standard photo or document format like a PDF or JPEG. At least one of them should work. Tell him to keep trying until he can read them."

I nodded and then concentrated. My thoughts were in the cloud within a moment. This was getting easier each time. I ran my consciousness up and cut perpendicular to the waves that mostly moved left to right and went straight up. I hit the accelerator and then thought of Kristopher's computer again. Like before, my signal went from fast to unmeasurable. It was like the speed of light without any light. I was just there. I was on the other side of the screen and sent out my first thought.

"Kristopher? It's Grey. You there?"

I didn't see him in his room.

I saw my words appear on his messenger. Within a few seconds it showed it had been read. I saw that he was typing something.

"Grey! I'm just down the street. Be right there!"

"Okay," I thought back.

Sure enough, he was running into his room less than a minute later. Must have been on his bike. He couldn't run that fast.

He jumped into his chair and started typing.

"What's going on, Grey? Everything okay there?"

"We're in trouble, but we have a plan," I told him. "Need your help, though."

"Sure. How can I help?"

"We have some documents. My friend Blue can't convert them. He wants to use software to turn them into JPEG or a PDF so we can read them. Do you have something that can convert that?"

"Of course, Grey. I have Paint and some basic software

for JPEGs and I have an online PDF converter from my school account. They give us some awesome software. It's pretty quick to convert."

"Blue, are you locked on to me?"

"Yes, followed you all the way there. Going to see if I can establish a permanent connection and we can talk to Kristopher without you having to jump up there every time. Oh, wait. Leo heard me and said we may need to get some kind of specific permission."

"From who?" I asked. "There's no active Council right now. Just keep it open and we can figure out permissions later if we're still around after all this is over."

"Good point. Sending the files now."

I felt a small surge pass through my head and something was stirring on Kristopher's messenger. It paused for about 20 seconds and a document came through. Then another. This repeated for the next few minutes.

"How do they look?" I asked.

"I'm trying the first one," Kristopher said. "They don't have any kind of extension so I'm going to try and open with both programs."

He hit some keys and started clicking and typing. "The PDF converter isn't working. It's coming back with gibberish."

"It may not be in English. I'm not sure what language it would be."

"Don't you all speak different languages down there?" he asked.

"Yes, but they explained we can all understand each other in our own native language. So Grim may be speaking Dead-anese but I'll hear it in English."

"Wow. Star Trek without the language translator."

"I never thought about it that way, but yeah. Pretty cool. There's a lot of strange and amazing things out here. I might be able to tell you all about them someday. If we survive this crisis, that is. Can you try the JPEG?"

He started clicking again. I figure he was trying some of the image programs. His eyes flashed as he concentrated.

"Yes!" he yelled.

"Did it work?"

"I think so. It's not English, but it looks like some kind of language. There are some drawings, too. Here, let me send this first page. If Blue says it's cool, then I'll fix the others."

He clicked the mouse and I felt the surge go backward this time.

"Blue, coming your way. Check if that works."

"Okay, let me process them back into the system. Can you ask him if he can send me the executables for his software, too? Not sure if they'll translate but worth a try. Just got the first file. Let me check... Oh, wait. Yes, I can read it!"

I hadn't realized the words must also translate to our native language until now.

"Have him get the others and see if he can send the main programs and anything else. Let him know it's like I'm on MS-DOS down here!"

I relayed the message, although I wasn't sure what MS-DOS was.

Kristopher started laughing. "Sounds great. Let me get these going. Won't take long at all."

He typed for about ten more minutes and sent a file every so often. I felt each pass through.

"That's the last one," Kristopher said. "Fifteen total. I'm going to send him the executables now. Don't know how this is compatible with his computer, but hey, when it breaks down to the lowest byte level, it's just a bunch of 0's and 1's."

"I'll take your word for it," I said.

Kristopher had been into computers since he could walk, almost. His dad was a programmer and taught him a ton. He was programming basic stuff when we were in second grade.

"That's it," Kristopher said. "All sent."

"Blue, are you done?"

"Yes, yes. We're done. Get back down here so we can go over these docs. Some great info here."

"I need to get back, Kristopher. Thanks for your help. This connection has the potential to give us a solid link to our worlds without anybody having to die. We'll see if it holds up. I'll come back if we survive."

Kristopher nodded and typed. "Be careful. I thought I lost my best friend and to have you back, in any way or form, I'll take it."

"I know," I thought. "I feel the same. Hopefully things will work out. Thanks, blood brother."

I left reluctantly. Kristopher was my best friend, but I had other friends and an entire Underworld to save.

I opened my eyes back at the library. Blue, Cal, and Leo were looking at the documents now showing on the big table.

"What do we got?" I asked.

Leo was moving papers around.

"When these things scattered they got all mixed up," Cal said. "I wish we could have gotten those last files I grabbed."

"If we had, they would have changed everything if they thought we knew their plans."

"The problem," Leo said, "is filling in the key gaps. We may learn some of what they are doing but will have to make some big guesses with what's missing. Give me a moment to sort some of the materials."

He had several papers, mostly with hand-drawn illustrations, on one side. Then there were small clusters of 2 or 3 pages each, and a few that were just single pages. He concentrated and moved a few more around.

"There," he said. "I have categorized them by the illustrations that refer to different parts of the Underworld. Some are quite obvious."

He pointed to a couple of them. "For instance, this is Oracle's castle, then there is my library and this is the original castle where the Forta leaders lived and where the big battle with Oracle occurred."

Leo moved his hand to the center pages. "This group has some consecutive pages. Those two were written in order. This last batch over to the right contains individual pages that do not appear to connect to anything else."

"You're the super speed-reader," Cal said. "What are they saying?"

"What I can tell you is that these point to a way to keep Grim away, but we knew that. The rest looks like a plan for them to take individual areas. Strategic areas. The library is one, which makes sense since they probably know we have a base here. However, it's not strategic. They gain nothing by taking it over unless they know about the lab somehow, but that seems unlikely."

"So is there something there we can use to form a plan?"

"Maybe. The issue is that these are mostly notes, and some of these pages contradict each other."

He lifted one of the singles and then consecutive sets. "This one implies they want to attack the Oracle's castle and destroy it, while the one over here says to leave it as is and take the Oracle to the Forta castle."

"It's like they're brainstorming," I said.

"Yes, they are discussing their options much like we are discussing ours. They want to hold on to the Oracle more than anything because that takes away a major obstacle. It's a two-in-one situation. They hold on to the Oracle, and they also incapacitate the Grim One. It's a smart plan, but we do not know when or exactly what they will do next."

"Then we take what they have," Cal said defiantly. "When we played a team with a great player, we concentrated on shutting that one guy down and the rest of the team would usually fold. If we could do it."

I nodded. "The Oracle is the toughest option, but the smartest. If we can save her, we take away the main piece in their plan."

"That all sounds great, but how exactly do we do it?" Blue asked. "She is in the most heavily guarded piece of the puzzle."

I thought for a moment.

"We have one element of surprise. Something that no one knows about except for me and Cal."

"And what is that?" Blue asked.

Cal looked at me and smiled.

"Brianna."

CHAPTER 6:
PLAN OF ACTION

Blue's mouth opened. "What do you mean Brianna?" "She's back," I said. "She's been keeping an eye on Andi and is at the Council Chambers. If we can figure out a way to get her to the Oracle's castle, she won't be detected. The problem is she can't fully form."

"She could be a good distraction. Like a first-pitch knuckleball. They'd never expect it," Cal said.

I agreed. "Plus, they're on the lookout for Grim. They already think we'd never try. It's still not enough. Even if we figure out how to get Bri to help us, we still have to find a way to free the Oracle. We might be able to thin the herd, but there are still a lot more of them at the castle, right?"

Blue nodded. "I was able to pick up at least a dozen figures. And it's possible there are more that we can't detect."

"I can still talk to the Oracle through the Underworld Cloud. If she knows what's coming, she may be able to help, too. Leo, do you have anything?"

"I may. If Brianna can create a large distraction, we can

make them think they are under siege by a small army and that could be enough to leave the Oracle lightly guarded. However, even with only one Forta there, we weren't able to stop them before, so we have to be creative if we are going to make it inside."

"Let me know if you come up with an idea," I said. "We need to get a hold of Bri again. She seems to be able to jump into different areas. Maybe I can reach her."

"Yes, we need Bri, but see if you can find the Oracle first," Blue said. "We still need to go through the rest of these documents. I'll check it out while Leo looks for his distraction."

I sat down in the chair and was back in the Underworld cloud within minutes. I wasn't sure how to find Brianna, but I needed to try the Oracle first.

"Oracle, are you still out there?"

I got a faint reply. "Yes, here."

Her signal wasn't as strong as it had been before.

"Why can I barely hear you?"

"More Forta have arrived. They dampen my signal since I have to hide it from so many of them. They're also depriving me of rest. I'm tired and it's making my mind weak. Hard to concentrate."

"We have a plan and I wanted you to know."

"No!" she yelled in my head. "They have brought in other races and as tired as I am it's possible my messages could be compromised. Whatever you need to tell me only do it at the last possible moment and in short bursts. Do what you have to do. Have you heard from my Grimmy?"

"Yes, he is okay. He's protecting you."

"I know," she said softly. "I just hope he can forgive me and himself. A Grim Reaper should never be in that position."

"Don't think like that, Oracle," I said. "He's a better

being for it. Otherwise, what would he have to risk his life for?"

She didn't reply.

"Oracle, before we can proceed, can you tell me where in the castle they're keeping you?"

"I'm on the same side as the training room now, but it doesn't matter. They keep dragging me to each side of the castle to wear me out, so no telling where I'll be. They do seem to be keeping me on the farthest ends just to drag me as far as they can."

Hopefully they maintain that pattern so at least we'd be able to narrow it down to one end once we arrived. That was enough for now.

"We're going to proceed. I'll contact you when I can or when it is necessary. You and Grim are the strongest people I know in this realm. Don't lose hope."

"Never," she whispered before she faded out.

I changed my concentration to Brianna. I thought of her in the Council Chambers but didn't fly toward her consciousness like I had with Kristopher.

"Bri," I called out gently, expanding my pulse to the Underworld signal Blue still had running.

Still nothing. Up to now, she had been fading in and out and appearing randomly. I expected she would still be at the Council Chambers but I wasn't sure. If if I knew where she might appear next, it would be much easier.

Wait.

I opened my eyes back in the library. Cal was with Blue at the table, looking over documents.

"Cal," I said.

"That was quick," Blue said. "How did it go?"

"It didn't. I spoke to the Oracle but am having a problem finding Bri. She won't answer."

"Then our plan is over. We need to try something else,"

Blue said.

"No, I've been thinking about the times she's appeared," I said. "Maybe she just needs the right incentive. Can you hook Cal up to me?"

Blue looked at me strangely and one of his eyebrows rose. "Hook up how?"

"I want to take his stream of consciousness with me. I need a strong signal that will make it seem like he's right there."

"Why me?" Cal asked. "I'm fine with you walking in the clouds without me."

"Trust me," I said.

He let out a sigh.

Blue grabbed an extra monitor like the one I had on my head earlier and quickly wired them together.

"Sit, Cal," Blue said.

Cal pulled a chair up next to me and sat down. Blue put the connected headsets on us and hit some items on his machine.

"You should have a connection now," Blue said. "Your streams should appear to be together when you send it out."

I nodded. "Once we're out there, send me the latest Council Chamber location."

"I've never done this before," Cal said, his voice shaking slightly.

I put my hand on his shoulder. "I'll take you through it. Just close your eyes."

I saw his lids shut and then I closed my own. I was back in the Cloud and alone. I felt Cal's presence next to me, still connected by my hand on his shoulder, and concentrated on his essence. I was able to lift it with me and then we were in the Cloud together.

"Feel strange," Cal thought but I could tell he was

saying the words out loud back at the library where his body sat.

"You can just think what you want to say, Cal," I explained. "You don't have to say the actual words."

"Oooh. This is pretty sweet. This is way different than hearing voices and signals in our heads."

"I'm going to take you with me. We're going to do whatever we can to find Bri and I have an idea."

"Sending you the new signal for the Council. It's moved again," Blue said.

I felt the pulsing to the North. I moved our signals toward it.

"This feels kinda funky," Cal said.

"Just wait," I said.

"What do you mean?"

I didn't reply and got us closer to Andi's signal. Hopefully Bri was still with her.

We got there within a few moments and I immediately called to her.

"Bri? Bri, please answer me."

Nothing.

"Cal, try calling out to her."

"Brianna! Brianna Angel," he yelled.

Blue yelled at the same time.

"Just use your mind," I said to Cal.

"Yeah, you just made me and Leo jump a few feet," Blue said.

"Sorry, guys," Cal said. "Takes some getting used to."

"Go ahead and try again," I said.

"Brianna? Brianna? BRIANNA!"

I sensed something, but it went away right after I felt it. Still no reply.

"I guess it doesn't matter," Cal said.

"Actually, I didn't think that would work," I said.

"You're here for Plan B."

"What is Plan B?" Cal asked.

"She showed up and broke through only after you were in trouble. You almost died back in the Grand Arena."

"Yeah, so?"

"So, best if we leave it at that. You'll be okay. I promise."

"What do you mean—"

I threw his consciousness straight down like a fastball that he so loved to talk about. This fastball, however, was probably ten times faster than anything he had ever thrown.

"Aaaaaahhhhhh!" he screamed. "What are you doing?"

"Cal!" I yelled. "Cal, you're gonna die at that speed! You'll hit the ground so hard your soul will be displaced! We'll never see you again! Someone save him! Cal!"

"Grey, what's going on! Is Cal okay!" Blue yelled.

"No!" I screamed. "There's no time to save him! He's headed straight for the Crystal of Truth! It'll rip his soul apart!"

Cal was screaming without taking a breath as his consciousness hurtled down. I shot down after him and saw his bright essence as he grew closer to the ground. The surface came up fast and a second before he hit the ground, Bri appeared and reached her arms out. She was left staring as Cal's bright consciousness flew through her hands right into the hard surface. She looked down, confused.

"Brianna," I said softly. "I knew you'd come for him."

"What happened? Where are you? Is he gone? He was heading straight into my arms! He was so fast I couldn't even see his body!"

"It's okay, Bri," I said in her head. "It was just his consciousness I sent down. I figured you'd be able to hear him since you're kind of between planes. I know you heard him somehow that first time."

"So he's okay?"

"Yes, he's fine. He's back at the library with Blue. I'm sorry I scared you, but I didn't know how else to reach you since getting back into the Council was going to take too much time."

"You did that on PURPOSE!" Cal yelled into my head.

I cut off the communication and turned back to Bri.

Her hands were shaking and she took a few moments to calm down.

"What was so important that you had to do that to me?"

"We have a plan to rescue the Oracle, but without Grim to help us, we need you."

"What can I do?"

"I'm not sure of the specifics, but you can get around here undetected right now. We need you to help create a distraction so we can try and save the Oracle before they hurt her. This should also help us get Grim back."

"But I can't even guarantee how long I'll be here," she said as she started to fade in and out.

"I know. We're going to have to hope you can do it long enough for a quick distraction. Leo's trying to figure out a solid plan we can use."

"What about Andi?" she asked.

"Andi seems to be okay in there. What happened after we left?"

"The Green and Pink Councilmen came in and saw the mess."

"Did Andi tell them she saw us?"

"No, she didn't, but they didn't ask. They recaptured the Keeper and he made it seem like he had just figured out a way to escape. They have no idea you were there."

"So she didn't rat on us? That's good."

"From what I've observed, it seems she will answer

when they ask her something specific. So if they didn't know you were there, they wouldn't have a reason to ask her. She seems to be unable to lie to them."

"Let's just hope they still have no clue," I said. "If they still trust that they have control over her, then that means she should be safe for now."

"What happens if they don't need her anymore?" Bri asked.

"I don't know, but there's not much any of us can do about it right now. Let's take this one step at a time. The first one is to try and rescue Oracle. I don't see a way to save Andi without her."

"Okay, I'll do whatever I can," Bri said.

"Can you meet us at the library?"

She nodded.

I let my conscience go and opened my eyes in the library where Cal was sitting with his headset off. He didn't look happy.

"Why would you do that to me?" he asked. "You didn't even warn me!"

"You had to be really scared. It was the only way I thought Bri would hear you. Whatever brought her to us, I think you're part of the reason she was able to get here. You've had a close bond with each other since the day we all met."

Cal's face softened a little. "You still should have told me. I knew my body was here, but you were talking about my soul splitting? What is the Crystal of Truth anyway?"

"It's from an old video game Kristopher and I used to play. Really cool artifact."

He looked like he wanted to hit me.

"Cal, what he did was smart. And he's not wrong," a gentle voice said behind us.

Brianna stood there, partially transparent.

"I thought about you on the other side. All of you, but especially you."

"Why?" he asked.

"Because I care about you, you dumb pitcher! You can read a batter but you have a long way to go with girls. Even the dead ones."

He smiled. "I've always liked you, too. Not that I hid it so good, but I wanted to tell you before you left. I just didn't see why if you were never coming back."

"I'm here now. Well, sort of here. I don't know for how long. What about this rescue plan?"

"I have something," Leo said as he pointed to a book sitting on the table.

"What is it?" I asked.

"The layout of Oracle's castle. I know you have been in there, but have you ever seen any of the rooms beyond the main floor?"

"Not really," I said. "We've seen a few doors and doorways but never been in any of them except the training room. You have the blueprints?"

"Not exactly," Leo said. "The Oracle is private and what I have was taken from the rooms and layout we knew when the castle was first built. I know she made her own modifications over the years so other than the entrance and main chamber, everything else could be different. What do you remember about what you have seen?"

"The stairs," we all said at the same time.

"They break left and right when you're facing her throne," Cal explained. "So it seems like the rooms go left to right."

"That is excellent information. Nothing behind it?"

"Not that I've seen," I said.

"That's good. That means we need to create a distraction on both ends."

"Why not just do it in the main chamber?" Cal asked.

"It's too open an area," Leo said. "We know Oracle's being held on one side."

"Hopefully I can find out exactly which side once we are closer," I said.

Leo nodded. "Once we know that, then we need the distraction. It should occur on the side away from the Oracle to draw whoever is there, and then another near her side but far enough out to hopefully draw more away but provide enough room to get to her. Then you only have to deal with whoever is left."

"They have to think there's more than just two or three of us," Cal said.

I nodded. "We need to keep it small like we discussed earlier. One person to create distraction number two, but if they think that's all we are, they won't take us seriously. There's probably enough of them to send out half and we'd still have too many to fight through to get to the Oracle."

"Can I help with my ability to appear and disappear?" Brianna asked.

"That is an excellent point," Leo said. "I think that will be a big help."

"What about the main distractions?" I asked.

Leo pulled a bag from under the table.

"I think this may suffice," he said as he removed an object the size of a watermelon.

It was metallic and had an opening in an oblong shape that sat on a tilted stand of some kind.

"What is that?" Cal asked.

"This is a purification cleaner and is normally used to clean off large structures, like my library. We have creatures and vegetation that build up on certain materials used for building. Once every few months, I take this and aim it at our walls. It shoots a strong pulse of air and purification elements that hit the surface and clean off the gunk. It's efficient."

"How is that going to distract anyone?" Cal asked.

"I believe Blue and I can work together to make this much more powerful. Powerful enough to break down material without completely destroying it. If we take a few of these and place them strategically around the Oracle's castle, it will seem like it's being attacked on multiple fronts."

"So you're saying you can juice it up and instead of cleaning the walls, it can destroy them?"

"We want to damage, not destroy. Damage that can be easily repaired later. I don't want a side of the Oracle's castle to fall, just to take some light damage to convince them we can destroy it. Also, the Oracle would be extremely angry with me if I blew up her castle."

We all nodded. The Oracle kept her castle in immaculate condition. If we all made it through this, I wouldn't want to be on her bad side.

"That takes care of one distraction. What about the other side?" Blue said as he started to look at the purification cleaner.

No one replied.

I considered what we had already seen and what else we could do. Then a thought hit me.

"I think we can distract them without having to damage the other side of the castle."

They waited anxiously for me to explain.

I took my time and told them my idea. If it worked, it could help get rid of more of the guards than expected. No one argued and everyone agreed it was our best shot.

CHAPTER 7:
PREP STEPS

We didn't know how much time we had but knew every minute counted. We spent the rest of the day preparing. It took Blue and Leo about three hours to get the purification cleaners ready. They worked to maximize the power of the machines. Leo was able to grab ten of the cleaners that we would strategically move and place. I had to contact the Oracle, but not until we were ready to move. Everything had to stay with us and hopefully, our enemies weren't ready to attack yet.

Cal helped me get my part of the plan together as Blue and Leo worked. Brianna popped in and out as we were preparing.

"Is there anything more I can do?" she asked.

"Save your strength, Bri," I said. "We need to be sure you're at full power once we're ready."

"Since you're here," Cal said, "What's it like on the other side?"

Bri looked down. "I can't really say."

"Is it against the rules or something?"

"Yes, but it doesn't matter. If I try to tell you anything about it, I can't. Watch."

She opened her mouth and said, "When you cross over the first thing you feel is jankerdoo. It's so agrapia!"

They looked at her awkwardly.

"Does your brain pop in and out separately from your body?" Cal asked.

Bri slapped his head.

"No, that's my point. Even if someone were to disobey and try to tell someone something, you would hear gibberish. That's actually the first time I've tried it, but I knew what would happen. From my perspective, I told you details, but that's not what you heard, was it?"

We shook our heads.

"It wasn't any language I've ever heard," I said as I continued working.

Bri disappeared briefly after our conversation and then appeared every so often to catch up with Cal. She asked about how things had been since she was gone and Cal filled her in on all the details. They looked comfortable with each other, even though Cal couldn't help throwing in a snarky comment or mentioning something about baseball.

After several more hours, we were done.

We met Leo and Blue back in the library.

"How's it going?" I asked.

"We just need to make some minor adjustments and go test this," Blue said.

About fifteen minutes later we were all outside with one of the cleaners and had it aimed at one of the far walls of the library.

"Ready?" Blue asked Leo.

"Just don't break any of my windows. I love my windows."

Blue adjusted the cleaner and pointed it higher. He stepped back and had his control pad in his hand. "Fire away!"

He pressed on the device and the purification cleaner shot out a quick succession of white objects that looked like thin socks that were balled up. They flew up over the windows and smacked the side of the library. The machine turned to the right and kept firing. It stopped as it went right and a cluster of the "bullets" hit a gargoyle. Pieces of the building and the gargoyle's left wing splintered and fell to the ground. None were big enough or close enough to hit us, but the noise was startling. It sounded like the entire wall might fall.

"Enough!" Leo yelled. "If I destroy that gargoyle, Koda and Pido may not be so eager to help next time. We can repair what's broken and I think we are good to go. Let's make these last adjustments on the rest."

"That was awesome!" Cal said. "But need a better name than cleaner purifiers. Kinda lame."

"They were not meant to be used this way," Leo said, trying not to sound offended. "What would you suggest?"

"Cleaner Cannons," Cal said without hesitation.

Leo's head turned. "You are correct. That is a much better and now appropriate name."

"How does a few hours of rest sound before we attack?" I asked.

Everyone looked at each other and we all agreed. We needed a little time to recharge, not only to give us time to review our strategy, but to also ensure Bri could fulfill her part. If she disappeared at the wrong time everything would fall apart.

Otherwise, we were as ready as we'd ever be.

We retreated back into the library and spent the next hour going over the plan again. Then we broke up and made our last adjustments. I sat in one of the reading rooms and rested. I tried to think of what other scenarios we may hit, but it was nearly impossible to know. The Forta were stronger than we were and we had no idea what other creatures would be there. We had no way of knowing how many more, either. They surprised us in Foglia Forest when I was strapped to the tree bridge and we had to assume there would be more unknowns we would have to face.

After a few more hours, the time was near. I went back to the library. Cal was the last one there, but we all arrived a few minutes before the time we had agreed on.

Bri popped up and looked more solid than she had since we'd first seen her.

"Now that we're all here, let's do one last review," Leo said. "We will portal to the Oracle's castle, staying as far away as we can to keep from being detected. We will move to the outer edge of the castle grounds where there should be fewer guards and will set up as fast as possible. Once we are done, Blue and I shall return to monitor from here. Then it will just be you three to carry out the rest of the rescue plan. Any questions?"

No one replied.

"Then it's go time!" Cal said.

"I'll try to contact the Oracle now to make sure we have a clear path," I said. "We'll move as soon as I return."

I sat in the chair and jumped into the Underworld Cloud. Blue was at his station, ready to monitor.

I searched for the Oracle and her signal was still there. It was the faintest I had ever sensed, but I had a solid lock on her.

"Oracle," I whispered in my head.

I knew there was no reason to whisper but with so much riding on what we were about to do, I felt nervous.

"Grey?" her voice said. She sounded weak. "I'm here."

"Are you okay? You sound tired," I said.

"Deprivation," she said. "They're still keeping me up and are now barraging me with sound to keep my senses weak. I can feel that it's working."

"We have a plan of action and are ready to move. I just need to know about their setup. I can only sense so much. Do they have outside guards or is everybody in the castle?"

I felt her latch onto my essence. "I'll show you while I still can."

My consciousness shot as fast as it did when I went to visit Kristopher. I saw a full spectrum of the castle and grounds. There were key guards on each side and at almost every corner, but only two outdoors.

"They only care if a castle breach is attempted. They aren't looking for you, just Underworlders like the Council or my Grimmy. Please tell me he's not coming."

"No, we know he'll give us away if he does."

"Good. I know it can't be easy for him to do nothing."

"We are coming for you. Just save what strength you have so you can help us once we make it in. If we make it in."

"I'm sure you've thought through your plan. At this point, none of us have anything to lose and time is critical. I can feel the anxiety in this castle. They are almost ready with whatever it is they're planning. We are fortunate they don't know about Blue's new connection to the Underworld Cloud."

"Thank you, Oracle. I hope we see you soon."

"Best of luck to you all. Be careful, but mostly, be brave."

I broke our connection and was back in my seat.

My comrades were waiting.

"We only have to worry about two guards on the

grounds. They are keeping close, but there are lookouts on each side of the castle. We have to be as stealthy as we can."

We all looked at each other. We each had slimeskin on to minimize our chance of detection in case they had any other telepaths present.

We were ready.

CHAPTER 8:
STORM THE CASTLE

We left the library and our loaded vehicle was waiting. This belonged to Leo's library and looked like a Road Warrior type U-Haul truck. It was about fifteen feet long and boxy with library books painted all around it. The rest of it was black and had thin looking armor.

"Where did you get this?" Cal asked.

"About two thousand years ago I was extremely frustrated with the lack of reading by the Underworlders. This was my mobile unit to try and spread books out."

"Did it work?" Blue asked.

"Total failure. The ones that regularly visited the library still preferred coming here, and I only converted about ten readers."

"It was a good idea, at least," I said.

We got in the truck, which was filled with the ten Cleaner Cannons, my boxes of supplies and a few miscellaneous items.

The truck entered a portal and we came out in an

unfamiliar patch of dry ground.

"Where is this, Leo?" Cal asked.

"We are a little over a mile from the grounds of the Oracle's castle. We cannot use any portals or signals that are too close. There's not much in this barren part outside her castle borders. This slimeskin may protect us from the telepaths, but since we don't know all the species of creatures that may be in the castle, any portal travel or loud noise could get us caught. Be careful and take your time. Rushing in won't help."

Leo opened the back of the truck and we started moving supplies. The Cleaner Cannons were the most cumbersome. Blue had set up water-based wheels that adjusted on rough terrain, so when we pulled them they remained steady, but we had to move slowly to avoid detection.

I wheeled one to its destination. We covered the right rear side of the castle where the Oracle was last being held and then moved to the opposite side. We set the cannons about 400 yards out on each side. I walked slowly and kept my eyes open. I eventually did see one guard walking around the perimeter and stopped until he passed. It took almost an hour to get everything in place. We returned to get our supplies and put them on the front and right side locations.

Once we had finished with all the supplies, we returned to the truck.

Leo and Blue got in.

"We'll be monitoring," Blue said.

"Only use your cloud connection if you have to," Leo said. "We have no way of helping you if this goes bad. We'll do what we can but if you get caught, there is no backup plan."

Brianna appeared for a moment.

"Good luck," she said, staring mostly at Cal. "I'll be ready."

Leo and Blue portaled back, leaving just me and Cal to finish the rest of the mission with Brianna hopefully in position. I moved to the right side of the castle where my supplies were and Cal positioned himself at the front. We were going to have to move fast once everything started.

I looked at the watch that Blue had supplied to all three of us. Two minutes to go. I tried to concentrate on my task. It was Bri and Blue's show to start. If there was such a thing as Anxiety of the Dead I was feeling it now. My hands were actually shaking a little, but then I thought of the Oracle and Grim, plus what they tried to do to Cal and Andi. I wanted to save Andi more than anything but the only way we were going to do that was if this mission succeeded. I was sure of that now.

Ten seconds. I closed my eyes and concentrated on Brianna and Cal and the mission. It was time for me to risk scanning for the Oracle. At this point, even if they reacted it would be too late. I eased in gently, and although the signal was faint, I sensed it.

"She's still on the right side," I said to the others in my head.

I felt a sense of relief that the Oracle was still where we hoped she would be as my timer hit zero.

Blue yelled "Now!" in my head and the first explosion followed. Blue, running everything from the library, sent Cleaner Cannon shots two at a time so they hit from the right and left to make it seem they were being attacked on both sides. I could sense the distress from the castle and zeroed in on what I could. Bodies were moving to both sides of the castle, but plenty stayed at their posts.

More explosions, then I felt Bri's essence. Blue and Leo had created a sort of action tiara for Bri. It had a juiced up signal built in that was supposed to allow me to jump on more easily and compensate for her fading in and out. It was like a telepathic camera so we could all see what was happening and decide when Cal and I were to make our move.

I popped into Bri's head and immediately felt the extra power from the tiara once she appeared in the castle. She was looking at four creatures near one of the explosions. They were looking up and surveying the smoke and pieces of the wall that had fallen. Some started heading outside. She appeared to them and yelled, "We're coming for you all!"

She then disappeared and reappeared in another corner just as one of the Forta and some other creature I didn't recognize reached out for her. I lost the signal as she disappeared but was able to maintain my view of what was happening. I couldn't send the view out to my friends.

Bri was in the back side of the castle now and there were three more creatures.

"You are going to die!" she yelled and just before she disappeared, I saw one of the Forta speak into some kind of communication device.

"They're in the rear of the castle, too! We're under siege!"

She repeated this four more times as the remaining shots rang out from the cannons.

I felt more of the bodies moving from each side of the castle and heard "Reinforcements!" at least twice.

There were still about ten bodies on my side and four of them moved closer to the Oracle.

"Oracle, be ready," I thought to her.

She didn't answer, but I felt her send me a pulse of energy which I hoped was to acknowledge she heard.

"Cal," I said to his head. "How many are coming out?"

"About six ran out of the front, but no one has in the last few seconds. You think it's time?"

"We're going to hit four guards with the Oracle," I told him, "And maybe a few more on the way. I'll send you the signal when I'm ready for you. Just don't wait too long."

"Okay," was all he said. I could hear the excitement and fear in his voice.

I waited ten more seconds. The four guards held firm and the other few were staying on the same side but scattering.

"Now, Cal!" I yelled.

I felt him run in as I stood by the Cleaner Cannon I had been near. I repositioned it.

"Go ahead, Blue," I said as I started running toward the castle.

The cannon shot more than twenty consecutive shots into one single location until the side of the castle wall gave in and left a hole in it big enough for me to fit through. The Oracle was just going to have to understand.

I ran through with a bag hanging over my back, the same type that Cal also carried as part of our supplies. As I entered there were already two Forta that had run toward the noise and another creature was just behind them.

My bag was already open and I pulled out my contribution to the second half of the plan.

I threw a softball sized container towards the guards and it exploded on impact. They were soon covered in ooze.

My idea was to pull off the ooze from the slimeskin and use it to cover the enemies. Once it started spreading on their bodies, I yelled, "Ooze Shock, Blue!" and Blue hit a button that electrified the slime that he had pre-loaded with metallic filings. Leo had told us the bugs were great conductors of electricity.

The two Forta and the creature with them fell immediately. I took a quick look into Cal's head and he had done the same for two Forta that had come towards him. I jumped past my electrified enemies and headed for the Oracle's room. Her signal had been weak when I scanned for her location, but now that I was inside the castle walls, I could sense her clearly. I also picked up that the four guards were still around her. Cal caught up to me just before I reached the room and we both stopped at the door.

I placed a Leo built explosive charge on the entryway and felt the bodies inside pulling up weapons, ready for us to breach. One grabbed the Oracle in front of him tightly. She didn't resist.

The door blew open and both Cal and I already had two softball ooze bombs in our hands. I ran in and threw my two blindly. They would head towards whatever body they sensed. Since Cal and I already had the full ooze skin on, they wouldn't come our way. At least that's what Leo assured us should happen. Cal tossed both of his and nailed two Forta directly on the head. Even with detachable arms, the boy could still pitch. Mine hit the third one on the leg.

I looked up to see where my last one had landed. It went straight for the Oracle's captor but exploded between them, spreading across her leg as well as the leg of her Forta guard. I finally got a good look and saw that the Forta was Voltaris, the leader of this uprising who we had seen on a video when he first captured the Oracle.

The ooze spread up both of their calves and thighs. The majority of Voltaris' torso was covered, but there was still plenty on the Oracle. I didn't want her to get hurt but if we didn't move fast, that would also leave the Forta leader to deal with and that might allow more reinforcements to appear. I had to decide quickly, but already knew the only option was to shock them both.

"Go Blue!" I yelled. The charge hit hard and the three other Forta went down. The Oracle and Voltaris shook and fell to their knees.

Cal and I moved in quickly.

The Oracle's hands and legs were bound. I pulled out a small sword-hilt dagger from my bag and cut the bindings around her wrists. Cal helped me pull her to her feet and just as we took a step Voltaris reached out and grabbed me by the shoulder.

"You aren't taking her anywhere, human!" he growled.

Cal grabbed him with his left arm and the Forta pulled it off a second later. Voltaris held up his arm to strike, but Cal smashed an ooze ball right over his skull.

"Blue, another!"

The shock hit Voltaris hard. Not much ooze was on his body but it was on his head. He shook and his head rocked back. He lifted his arm and got out, "Oracle is escaping, hit her with the dampening gel before she gets away!"

He fell on his back and kept shaking.

Cal and I pulled Oracle to her feet, but she couldn't stand. We dragged her out of the room and headed to the same wall opening I had come through. We turned a corner and I heard running behind us. We hit an open room and I looked back. Two Forta were following us at full speed. We weren't going to make it dragging the Oracle out. They were too close and moving too fast.

We had to fight.

I stopped and looked at Cal who was still holding his loose arm and trying to attach it. I reached in for another ooze ball but it was too late. One of the Forta raised what looked like a gun, but it was green and had a wide, round barrel. I didn't want to know what kind of bullet was coming out of that one.

He fired. An almost transparent looking gel flew out of it and straight for us. I felt the Oracle's hand squeeze my shirt and she threw me back.

"Move!" she grunted and used all her strength to push me.

I flew to the side and dropped my bag, hitting my head against a wall.

I looked up to see the gel they had fired hit the Oracle dead on. It covered her from her head to mid-torso and it absorbed into her body. She took in a hard breath and fell in a slump. I jumped up and didn't know what else to do. I charged the Forta, knowing we had to stop them before any more showed up.

They were both at least six and a half feet tall and I slammed my entire body into one while using my mind to heave blind force at it. It fell back but got up. I was so angry I couldn't concentrate. I wanted to throw something at it, but everything was moving so fast I didn't have a chance to react. It hit me back and I fell to my knees. I looked toward the Forta with the gun and he had it raised, about to bring it down on Cal. I was able to zone in on the gun and made it fly out if its hands before it struck Cal. Cal had one last ooze ball in his hands and shoved it into the mouth of his Forta, who was still trying to find his gun.

Cal flew past it and tried to come to my aid.

"Blue, again!" I thought, and this shock brought the Forta down immediately.

We just had one more Forta to get past, but I could sense others were on their way.

The Forta threw an arm out and hit Cal across the face, making him slide across the floor.

I felt a big pull from the Forta as something fell on his head.

Brianna was above me and had thrown a piece of the

ceiling on my enemy.

"We have to get her out of here!" I yelled, "More are coming!"

"Go! I'll take care of them," she said.

I nodded and ran back to the Oracle. Cal hesitated as his first instinct was to follow Bri, who had left the room to face the guards that were heading towards us.

"Cal, we need to get the Oracle. Bri is probably the safest of all of us. Let's go!"

He snapped back and ran with me. We grabbed Oracle, who was unconscious and pale. We dragged her as hard and as fast as we could.

We made it to the breach, got out of the castle and headed toward the clearing.

"Blue," I yelled into his head. "As soon as you can get a clear lock on us, get us out of here!"

We kept going. We moved past the Cleaner Cannon on our path when I felt a disconnect with the castle. I turned and saw several guards heading out of our breach towards us. We had a pretty good sized distance between us, but they were moving fast. We kept going until we were near the borders of the castle grounds.

"Grey, I'm getting a strong signal now. Sending you the car now!"

The ugly Robin appeared. We pulled the Oracle in and were gone the next moment. We appeared at the library seconds later. It hadn't gone perfect, but the Oracle was safe.

I just wasn't sure if she was still alive.

CHAPTER 9:
THE DOCTOR IS IN

We carried the Oracle through the front doors of the library and Leo was waiting. He led us to a room where there were some chairs and long couches, covered in a material I hadn't seen before.

We laid her down on the largest couch and it looked like it was covered in an alligator or lizard skin. I rubbed my hands against the strange material. It felt as soft as any feathered pillow I had ever touched.

"What happened?" Leo asked.

"They shot her with something. Voltaris called it a 'Dampening Gel.'"

Leo looked down at her.

"Oracle, can you hear me?"

She stirred. "Yes, but something's wrong. Grimmy. I need to see Grimmy."

"Can you call out to him?" I asked.

"I've been trying, but I can't see outside of this room."

"What do you mean you can't see?" Cal asked.

I turned on my senses. The Oracle's signal was weak. I

could only feel her presence in the few feet around the room. Whatever they had done to her, it seemed they dampened her telepathic abilities.

I leaned down to her. "I'll get him for you."

Her eyes opened as she stopped straining. They were large and round like the day we saw her when she thought she was a suspect. She looked frightened.

I jumped into the cloud and moved towards Grim. Hopefully he was in the same place.

"Blue," I called out. "I'm going to try and get Grim. Please let me know if you can get a signal on him while I'm out there."

I was in Tenebris again, although my last visit had been in the flesh with Cal. It was the darkest part of the Underworld and where Grim had chosen to stay to keep the Oracle safe. I had to be careful last time I was here, but I had no reason to hold back now.

"Grim!" I mentally yelled as hard and loud as I could.

"What are you doing?" he whispered back.

"The Oracle is safe, but something's wrong with her. We're in the library."

I felt him reappear inside the library an instant later. When I opened my eyes, he was standing next to me.

"What happened?" he asked.

"One of the Forta hit her with something he called a Dampening Gel and they had already been depriving her of any rest. She's exhausted, and her signal is weak. She couldn't even use her senses past this room."

She looked up at Grim and smiled.

"What did they do to you?" he asked.

"I'm sorry," was the first thing she said. "I compromised you."

"Don't worry about that right now," Grim said. "We need to know what they've done to you."

"Everything is dull. I don't know if it's from the deprivation or whatever he hit me with."

Grim turned to Leo.

"Any ideas?"

"This is new. I think we need to get the Doctor."

Grim nodded.

Leo raised his hands and clapped them together twice.

"Doctor, we need you," he said calmly.

A green mist appeared and a creature walked out. It was black and green and looked like it was covered in shiny lava. He was translucent. We could see some of his insides. He also had four skinny arms with six fingers on each hand.

"What is the emergency?" the Doctor asked.

"The Oracle," Leo answered. "She was hit with some type of sensory dampening gel and was rest-deprived for days. She is unable to communicate with her normal power."

The Doctor walked up to her and two of his hands wrapped around her head while the other two felt her pulse and pressed down on her torso.

"I will need to probe your insides. Is that acceptable?" he asked the Oracle.

She nodded. He raised one hand to her face and the other to her stomach. A single finger on each of the hands elongated. One went down her throat and another went directly into her stomach with a wet, popping sound.

"What are you doing?" Cal asked.

"He is the Underworld Doctor for a reason," Leo said. "He is able to see inside through his digits. Like an internal camera. She is not being harmed."

The Oracle writhed a little but didn't seem like she was in much pain. The Doctor's other two hands were still pressing down on her abdomen and various parts of her body as he continued to probe. His fingers then popped out at the same time.

"Other than exhaustion, your body seems to be mostly unharmed. I shall check your mind now. Are you prepared?"

The Oracle took in a deep breath and nodded.

This time, the Doctor used an elongated finger on all four of his hands. Two went into her ears and the other two went straight into the top of her head.

The Oracle started to spasm and now she looked like she was in pain.

"Do not be alarmed," the Doctor said. "Her mind is powerful and there will be some discomfort, but what you see is due more to her natural defensive mechanism. I assure you it is not as painful as it may seem."

He probed for another few minutes and then his fingers popped back out. The Oracle relaxed.

"How is she?" Grim asked.

"Physically, she is fine, but her mental state is not the same. Her essence is weakened. The dampening effect they used was to diminish her mental abilities."

"Can you fix her?"

"I do not know yet. She may be the most powerful telepath I have ever come across, but if there is a way, I will find it. I shall require more time with her."

"Understood," said Grim.

I signaled for Grim to come outside. Blue and Cal followed. I noticed a more transparent Bri trying to follow as well.

"Grim, now that we broke her out, we don't know what they'll do," I said. "I know they are plotting against us, but will they stay at the castle or come to get her again?"

"I would expect they will accelerate towards their ultimate goal, even without the Oracle."

"Bri said Councilmen Pink and Green were trying to get

a final plan together."

"Even with the Oracle's rescue, the Forta got exactly what they wanted. Whatever they've done to her, she has been eliminated."

"I can still hear you and I can still fight!" the Oracle moaned from the room.

"Get some rest and please let the Doctor fix you!" Grim yelled back.

"We have you back, at least," Cal said.

"Even with me, they outnumber us. I am going to destroy them, make no mistake, but even I can't do it alone. My guess is that the Forta will hold at the castle until the time comes to execute their plan."

"So the problem is numbers," I said.

"They have an army, Grey," Cal said. "They have the Council and took out the Oracle. If they stay in a different location, then we have to separate. Three of us breaking out the Oracle was one thing, but now we're talking about a straight up fight."

"Numbers make an army," I said. "We need our own army."

"Army of what?" Blue asked.

I looked at Grim.

"Now that we have you back, we may have a better chance of getting to the Council Chambers."

"How is that going to help?" Cal asked. "We barely made it out of there undetected."

"They think we'll come for Andi or the Council," I said.

"Yeah, what else would we go for?" Cal asked.

"The Keepers."

Grim nodded. "They have protected the Council all this time, with recent events being the only drawback."

"We got to them before," I said.

"Yeah, but now they know Bob escaped his room," Cal

said. "How do we know they didn't move him and the rest of the Keepers?"

"We don't, and they may have even upped the protection, but with Grim back, it buys us another option. We show that we're going for the Council and rescue them if we can, but our main goal should be the Keepers."

"Wait," Blue said. "Brianna, can't you just pop back in and see what's going on at the Oracle's castle and the Council Chambers?"

Bri was more solid. "I'm not even sure how I've been able to appear in certain places. Let me try."

She faded in and out a few times.

"I can't. I don't even know how. Before I was able to move around the Council Chambers at will, but I can't get back to it. Maybe they blocked me somehow."

"What about the castle?" Blue asked. "You were just there."

Brianna nodded. Again she flickered, but was still in front of us.

"Nothing," she said.

"Hold on," I said. "Let's go back to the Doctor."

We all moved back to see the Doctor. He was near the Oracle, watching her, but otherwise just standing there.

"Doctor," I said. "I know the Oracle is a priority, but can you take a minute to look at our friend?"

"Is your friend ill?" the Doctor asked.

Brianna popped in and out again as I pointed to her.

"You could say that. This is Brianna Angel. She was on the other side and came back to us, but she's still not completely here. She also seems to be able to appear in certain places, but not others and isn't sure why."

Bri held her form.

"You returned from the Afterlife?" the Doctor asked.

Bri appeared solid. "Yes, I felt a need to come back and

now I'm here, but something is keeping me from fully forming. I can only keep myself in full form for a few moments before I start to weaken. No matter how hard I try to hold myself together I continue to fade out until I can generate enough power to reappear."

"This is something I have never had the pleasure of examining or treating. It has been a long time since I have been able to state such a thing. If you will allow me to examine you, please attempt to hold your form."

"Yes, please," Brianna said. "Whatever you can do."

She appeared in front of him and the Doctor used four fingers from two hands to examine her through her eyes and ears while his other two hands checked her stomach and feet. As he was examining her, she faded. The Doctor's fingers looked like they spasmed as they appeared once her body disappeared.

"Incredible," the Doctor said.

Must have meant something to surprise the Underworld Doctor.

She reappeared partially and then fully. Once she did he inserted two fingers into her head. Bri faded out more quickly this time. After another two rounds of fading in and out, the Doctor retracted his digits.

"Did you find anything?" Brianna asked.

"From your physical examination, no. When you are partially or fully formed, everything appears normal and when you fade out, there is simply nothing there until you return. The examination of your mind and essence, however, yielded something. Something I have never experienced before."

"What is it?"

"I must check something first," the Doctor said.

He turned to the rest of us. Three fingers popped out of one of his hands, with one pointing to me, Cal and Blue at the same time.

"I must perform a brief examination on all three of you. Nothing as invasive as the others."

"Uh, I'm good," Cal said. "I already had a tree stick a branch up my nose. I don't need a finger in my head, too."

"Cal," I said. "It's for Bri."

"Yeah, it's for me, Pitcher," Brianna said through her gritted but fading teeth. "You know, the one who saved your life?"

Cal groaned. "Ugh. Not the guilt card. You're as bad as my Momma when she wanted a hug right after a game. Okay, fine."

I didn't want a finger in my head, either, but I knew it had to be done. I nodded.

"Blue, you good?"

"You kidding? As disgusting as this sounds, it's for science."

"Very well," the Doctor said.

He reached a hand in front of our faces and two fingers of each hand entered through our ears. It tickled, but his fingers seem to have been so thin that I barely felt it. The popping noise I heard was the only thing that made me twitch, but there was no pain. As quickly as the fingers entered, they came right back out.

"As I suspected. Brianna Angel, your essence is tied to four others. Four signatures that I am unfamiliar with and are not that of a typical Underworlder. These are three of them. I can surmise that you have another in your group that is the fourth."

"Andi," Brianna said. "The five of us all appeared here together."

"I am aware of some of your story," the Doctor said. "It now makes sense that the five of you would have a special connection."

"But what does that mean?" I asked.

"The reason she has been able to appear in certain places is that one of you was present."

I thought about it.

"That's right. Cal at the Arena. Andi at the Council Chambers. Then you were able to travel with us to the Oracle's castle."

"That explains why I can't go back to the Oracle's castle, but why can't I go back to the Council Chambers now if Andi is there?"

"The Council has their protections," Leo said. "It may be more difficult for you to return now that you are here, even if Andi is still there."

I thought about it. "If she were to come back with us and follow our trail to the Council, then she should be good, right?"

"I cannot say for certain," the Doctor said. "However, that seems like a logical conclusion."

"Doctor, can you fix her? I mean can you make it so she can stay here permanently?" I asked.

"Not at the moment. Her inability to remain may be a result of her crossing, and even I do not have that kind of power or knowledge. I would need time to examine her further and for considerably more time. However, the Oracle is my priority and from what I have gathered, you will need Miss Angel in your coming tasks."

"Yes, you're right," I said. "We do need her. Thank you, Doctor."

"Then let's get to another plan," Cal said. "Since Bri can't get there without us, we'll have to hope that the Council doesn't know that we were ever there."

"Yes, we need to get back there," I said. "Between us and the Keepers, we may have our army."

"They'll still outnumber us," Blue said.

"Yes, but the Keepers can cover a lot of ground. You saw how Bob moved. He'd be hard to take down."

"Let us get a coherent plan, then," Grim said.

Grim looked in on the Oracle and informed us the Doctor had resumed examining and monitoring her.

We moved to the main computer room and circled the table.

We updated Grim on our previous trip to the Council and how we got in and out without being seen.

"Even with the Keepers, assuming we can rescue all of them, it would be a big benefit to contact at least one of the good Council members. Let them know what we're planning."

We went through our previous steps.

"We will have to do this in two phases," Grim said. "The first will be to go in and determine if anything has changed and if we will still be able to free the Keepers. If that goes well, we can move on to the actual rescue and possibly contacting a Councilman."

Brianna appeared in full. "What about Andi?"

I nodded. "We need to try to save her, but she's the one I want to be most careful with. Once we can assess the entire situation, we can do that, but I want to be sure it's the safest option possible."

"But we don't know how much control they have on her," Cal said. "It's too risky."

"If the opportunity comes up and we can get her out, we can keep her at the library or hide her until we know for sure. I'd still rather have her here."

"If we are able to do this, there's not going to be much time to adjust. If Pink and Green still have a plan in place, they will be forced to execute it." Blue said.

"You're right, Blue, but how do we know they're not already coming?" Cal asked.

We all nodded.

"Good point," Blue said.

"There is one other problem," Grim said.

"What's that?" I asked.

"The Keepers duty is to obey and serve the Council. There is no guarantee which side they will lean toward with a fractured Council."

"Bob said the same," I said. "He understands what's happening, but couldn't guarantee that the other Keepers would agree with him. We don't know where the good Council members are, and they may be the only ones who can convince the rest of the Keepers that Pink and Green have turned."

"But they were imprisoned!" Cal said.

"Yes, but they still have their directive," I said. "We need to try and get a Council member freed to talk to them."

"There are many 'what if' scenarios coming from this plan," Grim said.

I nodded. "It's the best we have right now. Any other ideas on what else we can do?"

No one said much.

"We have to trick them," Cal said. "If they see us coming, we won't stand a chance."

I nodded. "Yes, to use one of your favorite expressions, Cal, we need to throw them a curve ball."

CHAPTER 10:
CHAMBER RAID

"There's not going to be any getting in and out quietly this time," Cal said. "The Councilmen will definitely know we're there."

"Yes, that's true. A full out fight or war won't be long after."

"Back to the slimeskin?" Cal asked.

"Yes," Leo said. "A fresh coat would be ideal."

"Even Grim is going to wear it?"

I hadn't told Grim that detail yet.

"I will not be wearing anyone's skin," Grim boomed.

I smiled. "As much as I'd love to see that, I don't think that's necessary. Grim can get in and out anywhere he chooses, right?"

Grim nodded. "Now that you can pinpoint the location of the Council Chambers, yes. Normally, this is the only place where I would not have free rein without the permission of the Council. Things are different now."

"We go in first, and Grim can appear when we need him. There'll be a point where it won't matter once they know we're there. Then we have to hope we have some luck and maybe some divine intervention for things to go our way."

"Nothing has gone completely our way yet," Cal said. "Look what happened with Oracle."

"Yes, I hear you but she is safe," I said. "Let's get these details worked out now. Leo, will we be traveling by gargoyle again?"

"No," Leo said. "It would actually be considered impolite to ask for a second favor so soon."

"Then how will we get there?" Cal asked.

"We will still be able to lock on to Andi," Leo said. "We needed the gargoyles to get you in and out of there quietly the last time. We still want to get you there quietly, but must risk your detection once you breach the chamber grounds. We will portal you there with your car."

"But they'll know we're there!" Cal said.

"That is a possible scenario," Leo said. "However, there were no Forta last time, just Andi and the two Councilmen with the imprisoned Keepers. From what happened the first time, they seemed quite occupied with their planning and never sensed you due to the slime."

"Won't they sense the car?" I asked.

"I suspect they could, but we can simply coat it with slimeskin as well. Although the car is not an organic creature, as long as the slime covers it, it should get you there safely. At least long enough to get into the Council Chambers."

"As long as they're not sitting there waiting for us, I guess," Cal said.

We spent the next few hours getting the pieces together. We tried to come up with more "what if" scenarios and to prioritize what to do in what order, but there were so many unknowns. I knew we'd have to improvise at some point.

We finalized what we had and decided it was going to be a challenge. Blue was also coming with us. We needed every one of us and Leo knew enough to man the computer station. Once we had the current signal, we should be okay.

We portaled back out to the Arena area and collected way more slime bugs than before in order to cover Blue and the Reliant Robin. We returned to the library and got to work.

After what seemed like an entire day had passed, we were covered in bug skin and the Reliant Robin was, too. I think the slime improved the color.

We were finally ready.

Cal, Blue, Brianna and I met outside the library with the Robin waiting patiently.

Bri was still fading in and out. She was a wild card since we only had her in short bursts, but we weren't going to succeed without her.

We portaled to the border of the Council grounds, left the car and snuck in closer. Bri immediately disappeared into the Chamber.

Nothing had changed since Cal and I were here. We found the tree and this time, the entrance was on the opposite side of where we had entered during our first trip.

Blue wasn't with us before. It was time for him to face the tree's test.

"Back so soon? How unexpected," the tree said. "You have someone new."

"Yes," I said. "This is Blue."

"What are your intentions?"

It was Blue's turn to face the nasal probe. I hated to admit I enjoyed seeing it happen to someone else. Cal snickered. Blue looked like he wanted to pass out.

"And your intentions, Grey and Calvin?" the tree asked

after Blue was done.

"What do you mean?" Cal asked.

"We already did this!" I said.

"Your intentions to enter the Council Chambers may have changed. It is my duty to be sure."

"My intentions are the same," I said. "To save the Keepers, the Council and our friend, Andi."

Cal was next. "I found out about my friend, Brianna. This time my intentions are exactly the same as Grey's. Do we have to get probed again? Really?"

The tree said nothing as two of its branches appeared.

It was not any more pleasant the second time around.

We were shown a new entrance brick and were back in the Council Chambers.

We moved quietly. Our first goal was to get to where the Keepers were being held.

We walked through the halls, but they were confusing since they were set up so similarly. There were no signs of any Councilmen, Bri or Andi.

As we got deeper into the maze of hallways, we heard some noise, but it was still far away. I recognized one of the rooms. It was the one that led up the stairs to where we had been before. I looked at Cal and we both knew where we were.

We moved toward the hallway with the Keepers. I wasn't sure if there'd be extra security or anything different since Bob had "escaped." We made it back to his room. I looked into the peephole. He was still there.

"What happened after we left?" I whispered.

"Returned me to cell. They knew not of your intrusion."

"They didn't try to add more security?" I asked.

"Yes. If I leave again, alarm goes off. Banshee snails around door, lock and peephole."

"What is a Banshee snail?"

"Small creature. For small spaces. If anything moves, they squeal. Loud. Piercing. Unique. All will know."

"It's okay," I said. "We just need to be sure we let as many of you go as fast as possible. We won't be getting out of here without them knowing, anyway."

We moved around the hallways to see how many Keepers were near. We found six.

"Where are the others?" I asked.

"West side of chamber."

"Cal, Blue. Go check on the last three and try to explain the situation."

They left as I turned back to Bob.

"Once you are all free, we need to know if all the Keepers will help us. What if the Council members order you to attack us?"

"I cannot know. I will explain to them."

"We're hoping to find the good Councilmen," I said.

"I will help. Pink and Green are traitors. Other Keepers must choose a side."

"Even though they imprisoned you all?"

"We serve Council. We do the best for Underworld."

"We don't have much of a choice. We need you."

"I am ready."

Cal and Blue returned.

"We found them and tried to tell the other three Keepers," Blue said. "Some weren't receptive."

I nodded. "It's time to bring in Grim."

"Grim One?" Bob asked.

"Yes, the Oracle is free and he wants vengeance."

I thought out to the edge of the Council. Grim was nearby, otherwise I wouldn't have been able to get my signal to him through the cloud. The Council was still strongly protected.

"Grim, come now!"

Grim appeared a moment later.

"The Keepers. We're about to free them but we don't know if they'll turn against us once the traitor Councilmen show up."

Grim nodded. "They already know I'm here. Let's see if this part of the plan works."

He moved toward the long hall and into their main planning room while I ran behind him. I hid in a crevice as I heard Councilmen Pink and Green arrive. As Grim entered the doorway, he transformed into a familiar robed figure with a red collar. He looked just like Councilmen Red, the Spokesman.

Councilman Green stopped. "The Spokesman has escaped! How is that possible?"

They ran into the room and I was able to sneak a peek through the doorway. Andi wasn't with them. Grim was there, but he faded through the back wall.

Green turned to Councilman Pink. "We need to check on the others to see if they are gone as well."

They raised their palms and a bright light beamed between their palms. Grim appeared next to me.

"It appears they bought it," he said. "Can you lock onto that signal?"

I searched. Before, I could only keep my signal within the Council grounds, but I was able to hone in on the energy emanating from their hands. It was shooting out in multiple locations, but two went to the same one. I followed it. I recognized the place immediately. The signal spread out and I followed a single strain, then I lost my connection and opened my eyes.

"They are all accounted for," Green said. "I think we have been misled."

"I think they're in Purgatory, Grim. At least two of them are. It was hard to find them, but I'm pretty sure the

Spokesman was there. I think they're trapped within the surrounding souls."

"Makes sense. More difficult to find them with so many souls gathered there. I'll return."

"Wait, did you sense Andi at all?"

"No, but I wasn't searching for her. These Councilmen are the priority right now, Grey. We can worry about her once we find the Councilmen."

I knew Andi wasn't the priority for the mission, but she was still a priority to me. I had to know if we could save her. The faster we found the Councilmen, the faster I could try to find her.

"I understand," I said. "They know we've tricked them. Now comes the next big risk. Grim, I couldn't get these doors open before. Bob had to swarm through the peephole, but that will take too much time since we'll be signaling the Council immediately that they've broken out."

Grim looked at me and pondered.

"All of you, show me your fists."

Blue, Cal and I looked at each other a moment and extended our hands and balled them into fists. We trusted the Grim Reaper with our lives.

He cupped his hands around mine and I felt a surge of power and heat. He let go and my fists were glowing like fire. He repeated the process with Blue and Cal.

"What is this?" Cal asked.

"You have a small bit of my power. It should be strong enough to take care of some troublesome doors. It will only last a short time, so get to it."

Grim disappeared and I moved back to Bob's cell.

I turned to Cal and Blue. "I'll take care of the Keepers here. Go free the other three."

I looked down at my glowing fists and tightened them.

"Stand back, Bob."

I pulled both of my arms back and then threw both fists into the center of the door at the same time. It shattered on impact, leaving splinters everywhere.

I released six other Keepers the same way. In each case, the banshee snails lived up to their name. For a few long seconds, their squeals made me hold my ears, but then they stopped. Their alarms had been sounded.

Blue and Cal ran back with the three Keepers from the west side. I felt the power leave my hands as our fists stopped glowing.

"That was cool," Blue said. "I felt like The Hulk when I was smashing those doors!"

All ten Keepers were with us now. Nine hovered around Bob as he tried to speak to them.

"They're going to sense us and will be here any moment," I said, feeling their presence.

The Councilmen ran into the hallway and stopped as they noticed the Keepers in the air.

Green wasted no time.

"Stop these intruders," he said.

Two of the Keepers turned to look at Bob and moved toward him, flanking each side, but did not attack. The remaining seven looked back and forth but held their ground.

"I command you to do your duty and attack! Lock them up in your cells!"

"They are traitors," I said aloud. "We are trying to rescue the true Council members that serve the Underworld and not themselves!"

Pink and Green looked at each other. They didn't try to attack, either, but they probably felt that they didn't have to with their bodyguards the Keepers present, even if they had imprisoned them.

Councilman Pink turned back toward the remaining

seven Keepers that hadn't chosen sides.

"Do your duty!"

Four more Keepers moved toward Cal and me. Bri appeared and caught everyone by surprise.

"Please don't listen to them!" she said.

The four Keepers hesitated but continued to move towards us. The two that had moved toward Bob had turned to look at us and now stood by Bob instead of against him. One Keeper grabbed me but Bob and his two Keepers were there to block him quickly. They were now facing off, three against four.

The three neutral Keepers saw the conflict and moved. They got between Bob and the Keeper who tried to grab me.

Councilman Green stepped forward. "Put him in a cell now! He is a danger to the Underworld!"

One buzzed by me and helped push me into the nearest cell while the other fought back Councilman Green. The door slammed and I was locked up. Just when it seemed the rescue was about to end before it had a chance to begin, I heard a booming sound.

"Stop!" Grim said in his scariest Death voice.

I couldn't see anything.

"Set them free!" he yelled.

I heard confusion and then my door opened. Bob was there. The other Keepers were hovering, staring down the hall. I looked to my left and Grim stood across from Councilman Pink and Green.

"Councilmen Pink and Green have joined with the Forta to overthrow the Council. They are traitors to the Underworld."

The two Keepers who had chosen to defend Pink and Green stood their ground.

"The Dead Club and the Grim One are traitors," the

Keeper nearest Councilman Pink said. "We do what is best for the Underworld."

The Keepers didn't move. Grim started to change. "I side with the missing Council members. The others are still out there. Why would they do this and imprison Keepers without any reason to do so!"

With each word he grew in size. He was over ten feet tall and his eyes burned fire. The Keepers moved back. Even I retreated a couple of steps and he was my friend.

The Keepers hovered but did not move or attack us again.

Bob spoke. "They are having difficulty complying."

Grim hovered towards the Councilmen and then looked towards the Keepers. "Do not interfere."

The Keepers held their position.

As Grim neared the Councilmen, they raised their arms and faced their palms toward him. Grim turned into a black cloud of smoke and in an instant each of his bony hands wrapped around both wrists of each Councilman. He held their hands high and a flame flew out of his mouth and entered each Councilman's face. Another shot of energy came from their hands.

Both of the Councilmen's mouths opened and they spoke in unison, but it was Grim's voice coming through.

"Grey, physically enter their signal. Find the other Councilmen."

CHAPTER 11:
KEEPING THE COUNCIL

The electric streams emanating from Councilmen Pink and Green's hands headed my way and I let them come.

The force hit me directly on the chest and my body felt like it was going to incinerate, but then I felt myself join the energy. It wasn't my consciousness this time, but my entire physical body.

I took a second to adjust and then locked my mental signal on the electric streams I was now a part of. I sensed all three Councilmen immediately and willed myself in that direction.

I reappeared in Purgatory, in the midst of the grassy valley where souls were wandering and waiting to pass on. I hadn't been in the midst of this since we fought Craver and Conniver, which seemed like it was a lifetime ago.

The souls were thick, but I passed through them quickly and gently, trying not to disturb them. The Councilmen were near and I had to hurry. I wasn't sure how long Grim could keep Pink and Green at bay or if the Keepers were still holding their ground.

I arrived at my destination. The three signals were in front of me, but I couldn't see them. There was a mass of souls huddled together. The Councilmen had to be in the middle of it all. I couldn't be gentle anymore. I used my hands to push souls aside. There was a wall at least three to four souls thick and when I got past the last line, I saw them.

Councilman Red, the Spokesman, was sitting on the ground with Councilmen Purple and Yellow on either side. They all were staring into nothingness and didn't notice me. Their eyes looked empty. I couldn't understand why the other souls were pressing near them.

I opened my senses and concentrated only on the Spokesman. It was something I'd never sensed before. His essence and signature were there, but it was chaotic. There were flashes of something within him, like random bursts of energy that were spread throughout his body.

Then I realized what it was. Souls. The same sense I got from the souls of Purgatory was coming through the insides of the Spokesman, but in a rapid set of flashes, like a bunch of paparazzi cameras flashing on a big movie star.

I checked Councilmen Purple and Yellow and it was the same thing. Somehow other souls were in them and their own senses were lost and confused.

I went back into the Spokesman's being. I knew what the souls felt like so I shut them out, pushing that signal aside until I only felt the Spokesman. I had him and connected.

"Councilman Red," I said softly. "It's Grey from the Dead Club. Can you hear me?"

I heard a grunt.

"Councilman. It's Grey Gomez. Listen to my voice."

"Grey?" the Spokesman said. "What? Where am I?"

"You're in Purgatory along with Councilmen Yellow and Purple. Pink and Green betrayed you and sent you here. It seems that they threw a bunch of souls inside you."

"So confused," Spokesman said. "Cannot see. Cannot feel anything around me."

"I think that's why the souls are here. Just follow my voice. I'm going to lead you out."

"Yes. I will follow."

I wrapped my signal around his and slowly led him out. He was still confused but clung to me. I left his body and his signal followed me. I let him come into my head.

"Can you see yourself?" I asked as I stared at his body.

"Yes, I see. The other souls are attracted to the souls within me and the others. They are blocking our senses and keeping us lost. This ends now."

I felt the Spokesman leave me in a powerful rush and I lost my breath for a moment as he did. His eyes returned to normal and he rose up in an instant as several blue streaks of energy shot out of his body. The energy re-formed into bodies as the souls returned to their normal forms outside his body. He was restored.

He immediately turned to the other two Councilmen and extended his hands with his palms cupped upward like he was holding something in each. The souls within his companions flew out and they stood up next to their Spokesman.

"Pink and Green are back at the Chambers, trying to get the Keepers to fight against us and Grim."

"Then it's time we return," the Spokesman said.

In a flash, all four of us reappeared. Grim no longer had a full grip on the traitorous Councilmen. The Keepers loyal to the traitors had moved with them and were struggling against Grim. Once we arrived, Pink and Green stopped and so did Grim.

The Council members then turned to each other to face off. They didn't start punching or attacking, but looked at each other hard like they were having the most intense staring contest ever.

I felt the psychic energy and it was an all out mental attack. The damage they were trying to inflict was to each other's minds instead of their physical bodies. I felt them straining and in pain but none would let up. Councilmen Red, Purple, and Yellow were weak from their imprisonment. Pink and Green were winning.

"Grim, why did you stop?" I asked. "What do we do? Should we intervene?"

"No, even I won't get involved now that they are all here, plus we could hurt them or maybe ourselves. Powerful energy involved."

"But the good Councilmen are weak," I said.

"Let it play out. It is their way."

Then a huge buzzing sound enveloped us. All ten Keepers formed a circle around the battling Council members. Bob started explaining the situation to the others, but the newly freed Keepers just looked at him. I could sense their confusion.

"The Council is split," I yelled at them. "Councilmen Red, Yellow, and Purple are trying to help the Underworld. Stand with us. They have an army and we need you!"

A few of the Keepers who had originally sided with the traitors or had been neutral looked at me for a few long seconds and then looked back. I hoped they weren't going to side with the winner as the good Councilmen were clearly losing. Their legs were dug down and their arms started shaking.

"Grim, we have to do something."

Grim took a long look. "We risk harming them."

"I don't think we have a choice. Even one good

Councilman is better than none."

Grim stretched his arms out and let out a banshee scream. All five Council members flinched and as they turned to Grim, he jumped in the air and came down on them, striking them all down at once. They fell in a heap, but Pink and Green jumped up and started to attack him. Grim flew back but looked more annoyed than hurt. I remembered only Underworld creatures could hurt each other, and the Council was the top of the chain.

Grim tried to move closer but couldn't.

I turned to the Keepers. "Help me save them!"

I reached down to try to pick up the Spokesman and drag him away. Bob came down to help me.

Three other Keepers joined in and helped us with the fallen Councilmen. Bri appeared and tried to help, too. We pulled as Bob kept talking to the other Keepers, but most of them remained where they were.

"Get the Council out of here," Grim said to me in my head. "I will keep them distracted until you are all out."

We rushed out of the hallway and back to the way we entered.

Before we left the chambers, I stopped. "Cal and Bri, come with me. Blue, get the Councilmen back to the library and the Doctor."

"What are you going to do?" Blue asked.

"I'm going to look for Andi. I don't know if we'll get another chance."

"Find her," Blue said as he rushed out with the Councilmen.

"Do we have time to look for her with everything going on?" Cal asked.

I looked straight at him. "I'm not leaving without her or knowing what happened to her. You can leave with Blue if you'd like."

"I don't want to be the bad guy, Grey, but what if she gives us away?"

"Are you saying you're scared of her?" Bri asked. "I thought you were a big, tough baseball player."

"It's not that!" Cal said. "She could turn on us right when we need her!"

"We don't know that," I said. "We owe it to her to find out. I'm going now. Go back to the library if you want. Bri and I can handle it."

He looked down. "I'm coming."

Grim was still going at it with Pink and Green. I had to let him know.

"Grim, we have been delayed," I said in my head.

"I know what you are doing. Just hurry up and find her. Without the other Councilmen here, the neutral Keepers are more likely to join against me, although they still look pretty scared."

"I can't blame them," I said.

We heard the fight as we rushed through the corridors. I stopped when we reached one of the open areas.

"Bri, go check what you can and I'll see what I can sense."

She nodded as she faded away.

I closed my eyes and threw my mental energy around the chambers. The fight was sending out the strongest senses, so Grim and the Councilmen were dominating my head. I couldn't rush this. I took in a few breaths and tried to block the signal.

"Andi," I thought to myself.

Still fuzzy. Maybe I needed to use her full name, even though if any of us called her by it, we'd usually get a punch.

"Where in the Council Chambers is Andromeda Lane?"

I pictured her and slowly spread my senses from my head in small bursts around me, avoiding the direction of the fight. I sensed Bri popping around, but no Andi yet. I thought about the room where they had all their documents during our last trip and moved in that direction, but again, nothing. I moved a little further out and then I sensed it. It was weak, but it was Andi.

"Bri, just outside that war room where they chased out Bob from before. She's close. We're on our way."

I took off without saying anything to Cal. He didn't hesitate and was right behind me.

We reached the same planning room and ran through it. I followed her signal down another hall a few feet past the room. There was another room without a door. There were more tables with boxes and odd artifacts along the walls. Bri was hovering and we only saw her back.

I rushed over.

Andi was in a heap on the ground. Her eyes were open and facing us, but they looked empty and distant. They reminded me of the lost souls I had just seen in Purgatory.

"Is she okay?" Cal asked.

"I don't know," Bri said. "She won't answer me."

I knelt down and touched her face. She was colder than normal and didn't react.

"Andi," I said. "It's Grey. I'm here with Cal and Brianna. Can you hear me?"

Nothing.

I reached down and lifted her.

"I got her," Cal said, reaching for her.

I knew Cal was stronger than me, even in the Afterlife, but I wasn't letting her go.

"I got her. Let's get her to the Doctor."

As small as Andi was she got heavier the further we ran. I never lost my grip.

We got out of the Council Chambers and rushed past the castle borders. Since we didn't have to get out quietly this time, we avoided bothering the tree and having to take another uncomfortable branch ride.

The Reliant Robin was waiting.

"Drive, Cal."

I carried her into the passenger seat with me as Bri jumped in the back.

"We got her, Grim," I said just before we disappeared to the library.

I rushed her to the Doctor's room where he had the Oracle. The Council Members were each on a table in the same room. They were still. I found an empty table and laid Andi on it. She was unresponsive, but I remembered what Cal had said. We needed to be careful with her until we knew what kind of state she was in.

"Bri, can you watch her, just in case?"

She was only half in but nodded.

I then realized that the Doctor and Leo seemed to be having a discussion and it didn't sound friendly.

Cal and I moved towards them.

"What's going on?"

"I called him before Blue arrived with the Councilmen," Leo said. "He won't treat them."

The Doctor looked flustered as he turned to me.

"What's wrong?" I asked.

"I am only allowed to examine them under their strict orders."

"They were just attacked!" Cal yelled.

"I am unsure of the protocol," the Doctor said.

"On the way over here, the Spokesman was able to tell me to tell you it was okay to work on them all!" Cal said.

We all turned to look at him.

"He whispered it to me. You can blame me if they say anything. Now help them!"

The Doctor nodded and his fingers were up the noses

and insides the torsos of each Councilman within the next few seconds.

"They are weak and damaged," he said.

"But they're alive?" I asked.

"Yes, they are alive. They are mostly self-healers and other than some minor issues in the past, I have never had to heal them. I do have something that will help. They require an energy healing and it will take time for that to complete. Their physical wounds I can address quickly."

His hands went into a pouch he had by the table. He rubbed a grayish paste on several visible wounds. He then pulled out three golf ball sized spheres of energy. They didn't make noise or crackle like electricity or lightning, but just pulsed. He placed one on the center of Red's chest. It slowly lowered into his skin until it was completely through. His chest glowed and then his entire body was pulsing slowly. The Doctor repeated the process with Yellow and Purple.

"They require time."

"Time is something we may not have, Doctor," I said.

Bob appeared in the room.

"What happened?" I asked.

"The chaos continues at the Chambers," Bob said. "The Grim One asked me to return and three Keepers have joined us. Will be along shortly."

"At least we have an army," Cal said.

"What army?" I said. "We have four Keepers, Grim, us and no Council Members. We need them back if we have any shot of defending ourselves."

"There is more of a chance than before you left," Leo said. "Blue's working on strengthening the communication system. We will be more prepared and have more options now. Relish the small victories."

I nodded. "Yes, I know you're right, Leo. We are better

off than before. We just don't know if the Council, Oracle, and Andi will be healthy enough. So many unknowns."

"In my experiences with Underworlders and history, I believe there is no way to know every possible outcome or plan for every situation," Leo said. "Grim once mentioned how some humans meet him after fulfilling every goal they set out to accomplish in life, but most never even got started. I think we fall somewhere in between."

I got it. Not knowing Andi's condition was frustrating. It was time to move on and plan. I couldn't control much else.

"What about the remaining Keepers, Bob?" I asked.

"They could not choose. They will not stand against us. Will remain neutral."

I felt a little better. "As long as they're not there to fight against you, Bob, I like our chances a little more."

"I am the better fighter. I would defeat them all in combat."

I smiled. He didn't sound arrogant or boastful, just stating it as a fact.

"Then we are fortunate you chose our side. I know it couldn't have been easy."

"After spending time observing I understood. Pink and Green had no reason to imprison us. They treated me like enemy after you freed me. Choice not difficult. I have been given more freedom with you and your group. Fortunate my closest allies joined us. What do we do now?"

"We have to go to war," I said. "There is no other choice. Now that we've broken out the Oracle, Andi and your Keepers, they have to attack or expect that we will. We don't think we have more than a day. If even that."

"Then we must prepare," Bob said.

"Yes, but we also need to be sure we have everybody at full strength. They outnumber us, but if we can get these

Councilmen along with Oracle and Andi, we'll be stronger."

"Understand," Bob said. "We will be ready."

I moved back to the Doctor, who was observing his Council patients.

"Doctor," I said. "I brought in one of our members. Can you take a look at her?"

"This is the one that was suspected to be a traitor?" the Doctor asked.

"Yes, but I don't think she had control of herself. She wasn't responding when we found her."

"The Council is the priority, but I am only monitoring. I can spare a moment.

He moved towards Andi who hadn't budged from her position since I had put her on the table. Bri was still hovering near her.

The Doctor examined her and spent more time in her head than he had with anyone else before his fingers popped out of her skull and face.

"Physically, she is fine, but mentally, she is empty."

"What does that mean and what can we do for her?" I asked.

The Doctor didn't respond right away.

"It was the two traitors who did this to her. This is beyond my help as it is most likely a Dommerian Council ability I am unaware of. If I can get any of these Councilmen healthy enough to take a look, they may be able to help more than I can."

"Do you think any of them might be ready soon?"

"I do not know, but they are the priority. As we do not know what her condition is or what she may do, we should restrain her," the Doctor said.

"No," I said.

"We don't know what state she's in, Grey," Cal said in a

soft voice. "I don't want to do it either, but until we know, we need to play it safe."

I looked at the Doctor. "Do you have something that can knock her out until we can talk to one of the Councilmen?"

"I would rather not do so in case she responds normally. I would prefer to restrain her if she is a risk."

"I have an alternative," Leo said as he left the room.

He returned a few minutes later and lifted a transparent bottle with a label on it I couldn't read. It was filled with a clear liquid.

"This is a gravitational suppressor. It will keep her from getting up without having to bind her arms and legs."

"What's the difference?" Cal asked.

"She will be able to sit up, but the gravity in the bottom part of her body, especially her legs, will be increased exponentially and she won't be able to lift them to get off the table. It is easily reversed."

We looked at each other and no one objected.

"Okay," I said. "That sounds better."

Leo moved toward Andi and raised her hands so they were crossed over her chest. He poured some of the liquid on the table on either side of her legs. It spread like thick water and wrapped around her body to the edges of the table. Once it settled, it hardened into a gel. Leo popped a finger into the gel and it stuck briefly, like touching slime.

Grim reappeared. He was a little disheveled as his robe was bunched up and his hood was off.

"What happened?" Cal and I asked at the same time.

"Once I knew everyone was here, I let the battle go on a little longer. They are angry but had no way of defeating me. Once they realized you were all gone, they disappeared."

"Do you know where they went?" I asked.

"I would expect they rejoined the Forta."

"Back at the Oracle's castle?" Cal asked.

"No, I stopped there first to see where they may be. They've abandoned the castle."

"We forced their hand," I said. "They know they have to attack and they also know the Oracle and Council members are weak. We need to move quickly."

"I agree," Grim said. "How is the Oracle?"

The Doctor looked up. "She is healing steadily now that she is resting. She will be physically back to normal within a few hours, but mentally, it will take longer for her telepathic and telekinetic powers to heal."

Grim looked down.

"She's going to be okay, Grim," I said.

"I know, but she won't be the same."

"Then we need to stop sitting here," Cal said. "If we have a fight coming, we need to get ready."

CHAPTER 12:
COUNTDOWN

"Yes," I said. "Nothing went as planned, but we have almost everyone here. We can assume they will be coming, but we need to take the fight to them. First, let's find out where they are and get a basic plan ready. If we can figure out a way to get Bri to transition over, that would be a huge advantage. We need everyone and we need to move fast."

We moved to the war room where Blue was on his machine.

"Blue," I said.

"I know what you're looking for," he said. "The Council members moved out of the chambers and I tried to detect where they are, but I have nothing."

"Grim thinks they are all together now," I said. "The question is where. They have to be preparing an attack."

"I don't believe so," Grim said. "The most logical thing would be for them to wait for our attack unless they think we pose no threat. They know the area and also know we have to take them down, not the other way around."

"Yup," Cal said. "Home field advantage."

Grim nodded.

"I do agree," Leo said.

"But where would they be based?" I asked. "We have to know where they are if they are waiting for us to go fight."

"They may reveal themselves once they are ready," Grim said.

I thought for a moment. "We need a solid strategy. What are their weaknesses? We already know the Council has their mental abilities but don't pose a physical threat. If the other Keepers remained neutral then we have an advantage there. What about the Forta? What kind of weaknesses do they have?"

"They do not have many," Leo said. "During the Revolution we outnumbered them and the Oracle used her skills to defeat the leader. We no longer have that advantage."

"What about the other creatures?" Blue said. "We saw different races there."

"Yes, it is an excellent strategy for them to use different beings," Leo said. "We need to deal with multiple levels of strength."

"We all have our strengths," I said. "We just need to figure out where to best match everyone. If we evaluate the type of creatures we have to face, then we can plan how to best match theirs. We can put the physical against the physical, the mental against the mental."

"I will go against the largest threat," Grim said. "No one can escape Death."

"That is not always true," Leo said.

"What do you mean?" Cal asked.

"There are the Underworlders like the Forta, the Oracle and Grim. Since a true death cannot typically affect them and they must be destroyed into particles like what the

Oracle did to the Forta before, it poses a more difficult situation if there are many enemies. Based on what we've already seen, I believe this will be the case."

"Then how do we stop them?" I asked. "Or at least slow them down."

"Everything has its weakness. The Oracle had her power, which she will not have in time, it seems. In their case, aside from Underworld force, elemental energy would be the best."

Fire and water. I looked around the room. "Bri?"

She appeared.

"Are you able to shoot fire?"

She looked down. "I haven't tried. It is taking all that I have just to try to keep myself here."

"Can you?"

"But please," Leo said, "Aim over there."

He pointed to a corner of the room with various metal objects lying around. "That metal is fireproof."

She drifted to the area and took in a breath. She let out a thin shot of fire, but it quickly faded along with her body.

"Oh, my!" she said.

"What's wrong?" Cal asked.

"When I shot the fire out, it seems to drain me and I'm fading faster than I have been."

"Leo," I asked, "Is there any way to help keep her here?"

"I'm not sure. We've had beings return from the other side, but never someone who's half in and out and definitely no one who could breathe fire."

He looked to the air. "Plane coexistence," he said and then threw in a few more words as more than a hundred books flew into the room and hovered over our heads.

"Between worlds. Crossing over. Corporeal problems. Plane transference."

Books continued to zoom in and out until only four

were left. He raised his hands and a book came down. The pages flipped, then he repeated the process with the other three books.

"I have not had to say this in a long time, but I have found nothing," he said after finishing the last book. "It is beyond the knowledge of the Underworld facts. The Council may know more, but this is something that has never been encountered."

"We'll take Bri however we can, then. If her fire can't help, then we'll have to hope our combined abilities will counter them," I said. "Grim takes on the Forta who seems to be the most powerful. If we can get Andi involved, she'd be critical."

"I wish I had their powers," Cal said. "Flying arms and legs aren't as powerful as water, snot and especially fire."

"You have accuracy," Grim said. "When the need for an accurate strike is necessary, you would be the one I'd trust most."

Cal smiled.

Who knew the Grim Reaper could give a pep talk?

"Okay, we can't plan for everything, so we need a strategy. There are at least four or five Forta. Grim, even you can't handle them all."

"The Oracle is the one who defeated them before. I'll take her place and will face however many I must."

"You do not need to replace me," the Oracle's soothing voice echoed from the doorway.

She was standing there looking at us. She looked like she had just woken up from sleeping for a month, but otherwise okay.

"What are you doing?" Grim said. "You should be resting."

"I've rested enough. We need to stop them or the entire Underworld could be destroyed. I won't be on the sidelines."

"Has the dampening effect worn off?" Cal asked.

"No, and it will take days for it to wear off."

"Then how are you going to beat them?" Cal asked.

"Even without my telepathic abilities, I can still fight." Grim nodded.

"She is correct," Grim said as he touched his chin. "She has a mean right hook."

She walked towards us. "Everyone good with that?"

I smiled as she stopped in front of us. "No doubts here. We need you and you have the most experience."

Behind the beauty and the mesmerizing looks was still the core of who she really was. I knew the Oracle was one of the toughest beings I had ever known. Considering Death was my friend, that was saying something.

"How is Andi?" I asked her.

"I checked on her before coming in. She is still out of it, but I may be able to reach her."

"What do you mean?"

"She is physically there. Even with my diminished abilities I was able to get into her head while I was next to her."

"The Doctor said we would need a Councilman to help her," Cal said.

I had a thought. "Oracle, we need every one of us and we need to know if Andi is still compromised or not. You remember when I was in the cloud and you helped boost my signal?"

She nodded.

"Do you think we can combine to try to help her, even without a Councilman?"

She pondered for a few moments.

"I think it's worth a try. They have a lot more beings than we expected. We need everyone in this thing or we won't stand a chance. We will be more powerful than most creatures, but with so many, we still need to stop them.

"Then let's not waste any time. Leo's doing some research and if we can get Bri and Andi involved now that you're here, we will be that much better."

"Come with me," the Oracle said.

CHAPTER 13:
FANTASTIC VOYAGE

We left the room while Blue stayed behind. Cal followed us and we moved to the room where Andi and the rest of the patients were. The Doctor was checking on the three Councilmen.

"Doctor," I asked. "Is Andi healthy enough for us to try and help her?"

"Help her how?" he asked. "I've done all I can for her."

"Oracle thinks we might be able to reach her mind."

"But how? Oracle, you are in a weakened state and I do not recommend pushing yourself."

The Oracle turned to me and grabbed my hand.

"Grey may surprise you," she said. "I think we can do this together."

The Doctor nodded. "Physically she seems to be sound. I don't see how it could bring her any additional harm."

Andi was a few feet from the Councilmen. The Oracle kept her grip on my hand and put her free palm on one side of Andi's face. She guided me to go to the other side of Andi and I placed my free palm on Andi's cheek.

"I'm not sure what to do," I said.

The Oracle was in my head. Her signal was weak, but I heard her clearly.

"This will be something new, Grey," she thought to me. "You've seen through other's eyes, but we're going to travel into her consciousness. In my current state, I can only get so far in. It will be unusual at first, but just like you can sense where some people are, you will sense an additional energy inside of her body and inside of her mind. We'll move slowly."

I took in a breath. "If there's any chance to bring her back, I'm in."

Oracle squeezed my hand a little harder. I felt her essence, like a small ball of energy, emanate from her head and then hover right in front of me. It buzzed near my eyes and beckoned me to follow. I was able to move my consciousness, just as I had when traveling to the cloud, and I followed her slowly in front of Andi's face.

I could see Andi's clammy skin and followed the Oracle in through her forehead. Nothing popped or broke, we just went straight through.

I felt my knees buckle as we entered.

"It's okay," the Oracle said. "That's her essence. It's different once you're in this far. Do you sense her?"

I could feel that it was Andi as if she was next to me talking or fighting. It was the sense of someone standing next to you, except it was like she was standing on my shoulders with no weight.

"This is her overall essence. Part of her soul and her being," the Oracle said. "We have to go deeper."

She started to move further into our almost glowing surroundings, like the videos I had seen in science class of diving into a molecule to see the even smaller protons and neutrons that were deeper within. Like a subatomic galaxy.

We moved in and I felt myself shaking. This was something different.

"What is this?" I asked.

"We are traveling into her consciousness. Almost into her soul. Normally, we would have felt her life source by now. We'd be able to hear her thoughts or feel her emotions, but right now there is nothing. We have to keep going."

It took me a moment to adjust and gather myself. We hadn't moved.

"I'm ready, Oracle," I said.

"Yes, I know. I can't go any further."

I honed in. The Oracle's signal was weak and I felt her losing her grip.

I took in a few deep breaths. I felt her essence starting to diminish, then eased mine closer to her until we grazed each other. I felt a spark as our essences touched and willed energy toward her. She immediately got brighter.

"Together," I said.

Our energy joined and I felt a surge of power. I couldn't speak and thought I might lose control, but then it subsided. "Are you ready?"

As I spoke, in my head, the voice was a combination of my voice and the Oracle's. Like we were both reciting the same poem.

"Yes," we said together. "Proceed."

We moved deeper into Andi's essence. Everything around us was black and then we heard a buzzing sound that turned into a stream of lights waving slowly in the darkness. I heard something like radio interference as we neared and then it sharpened until we heard a soft voice.

"Who's there? Please let me go."

It was Andi's voice.

"Andi," we said. "It's Grey and Oracle. We're inside

your head and trying to help you. Your body is on a table in the library, but we need to heal your mind."

"Grey? Grey, I'm so sorry. I didn't want to hurt you. Any of you. But I..."

"Andi, it's okay. We know the Council members did this to you. You couldn't help it."

"But it was still me! I helped them and this is my fault!"

"No," we said. "They did this to you and it's their fault. We need you to help us stop them and we're trying to get you out."

I felt our shared consciousness try to expand and grip Andi. The darkness flashed into lights. Floating green and blue balls of light that looked like stars in the sky were all around us.

"She is everywhere," the Oracle said. "She should be centered, but I cannot lock on. There is nothing to grasp."

"What does that mean?" Andi said. "I'm going to be stuck inside my head forever while my body is a zombie being controlled by someone else?"

I felt her distress. She had no hope. She had been in this state for days and I could feel that she saw no way out. That her life was over. She was frustrated and angry.

"Andi, you have no way to control this. Let us keep trying."

I tried to concentrate even more, but nothing changed. We were here and our signal was strong, but I didn't see any way to connect to her or a way to help guide her. I could isolate a piece of her floating essence, but it was like trying to grasp particles of colored air. Even together, we couldn't isolate anything. Whatever the Council jerks did to her seemed to be stronger than even our combined effort.

Wait. The Council jerks.

"Oracle, would the Council have been able to do this

without an object or anything? Was it only with their minds?"

"I would expect so. They are powerful alone, but Councilmen Pink and Green could have combined to make whatever they did even stronger."

"Andi," I said. "We'll be right back."

"Grey, please don't leave me alone again!" she said, her voice quivering. "What if you don't come back and I'm lost in here forever?"

"I will be back," I said. "I promise."

I felt her calm down a little before I let myself go, taking the Oracle with me. Our eyes opened together and we stared at each other as Andi still lay motionless with our hands on her face.

"What are you doing?" the Oracle asked.

I moved towards the Councilman nearest me. The Doctor was checking on him.

"Doctor, how are they doing?"

"Getting stronger," he said. "They should all be fine soon."

I put my hand on the Spokesman's arm. I felt the strength in his essence. Even injured, he was emanating power.

"What are you doing?" the Doctor said.

"The other Council members did something to Andi to suppress her essence and get her to follow them. That means all the Council should have that same power. I think if we bring even one Councilman's consciousness with us it will allow us to free her."

"Absolutely not," the Doctor said. "It is my sworn duty to protect the Council over all others!"

"You just said they were fine," I answered. "Oracle, if they are physically fit, there isn't much risk, right?"

She thought and nodded slowly. "Normally I would say

there is a minimal risk, but the ability to free what has been done is an unknown. I just don't know."

"Then it's settled," the Doctor said. "You will not risk the Council. They are more important than any other beings here."

I took a long look at the Doctor. "I don't think you understand, Doctor. Andi is more important to me than almost any being I have ever known. She was my first friend when I arrived here and she is a part of me. I recently doubted her, even though it was only for a brief moment, but that won't ever happen again. She's... She's family."

"That is inconsequential," the Doctor said, raising his voice. "I forbid it."

"You definitely don't understand, Doctor," I said as I felt my power surging. "I'm not asking for your permission."

The Doctor rushed backward as I threw my power towards him. I expect he would have gone through the wall had I not felt the Oracle pull me back. Instead, he had to catch himself to regain his balance.

I stared straight into his eyes. "Right now, Andi has priority. I take full responsibility, and your protest has been noted and will at this point be ignored. Do not interfere."

I reached down and grabbed the Spokesman's hand. I reached back and grabbed the Oracle's palm and we formed a small chain as she put her free hand back on Andi's face. I fell to my knees and I reached into the Councilman's head and the three of us dove back into Andi's mind.

I felt like I had grown twenty feet tall and had a wall of concrete surrounding me. With the combination of our three essences together, it was like I was a living boulder crashing through a spiderweb. There was no resistance as we flew through her in a blaze.

"Slow down, Grey!" Oracle said. "You could scatter her even further if we come in too fast with this much power burning."

I tried to slow down, but it was difficult to control. "Help me, Oracle."

"I'm trying, but you're running this train. I'm too weak."

"Then what do I do?"

"Try to wrap around us. Like you're trying to give yourself a big hug, but then grip down as tightly as you can!"

I tried to wrap my thoughts around our combined, powerful energy. I got about halfway around and had to push to get more of a grip, then felt my neck and face straining in my body even as I was disconnected. I was able to get more of a sense of just how big and powerful we were.

"It doesn't matter how big it feels," the Oracle said. "Use your mind to see it smaller. If it looks like a giant rock, turn it into a pebble."

I wasn't sure how to do that. I tried and pushed even harder. Instead of thinking how I was going to wrap around, I concentrated on making us smaller. It started to work. As our sphere reduced, the size seemed less intimidating. I kept going smaller until I was able to wrap myself around us all. I felt more like a huge balloon filling and releasing air than a pebble, but it was manageable. I felt my stress ease and I had my arms completely around myself in a big self hug. I squeezed harder and then felt everything ease. Andi's lights were ahead. Had to move faster.

And then I felt us slow down, like gently easing on the brakes of my bike. No screech, just a nice slowdown.

I felt Andi again.

"We're here, Andi."

"You came back!"

"I promised you we would. We have some help, too."

"Oracle," Andi said. "I'm not sure how but I can kind of sense you better than before. Are you okay?"

"I'm weakened. They attacked me, too, but Grey used another force to help us."

There was darker-green energy around us.

"No!" Andi yelled. "They're here, Grey! The Council!"

"It's all right, Andi. This is Councilman Red. The Spokesman. He was also imprisoned. Only Pink and Green have gone bad. The Spokesman is knocked out and healing right now, but we were able to use his energy to get to you. I'm hoping combined we can get you out."

The dark energy started pulsing a little brighter.

"I am here," the Councilman said gently. "Where am I?"

"Spokesman," I said. "I'm sorry but I had to use you to help me save Andi. Councilmen Pink and Green had her under their control. Her consciousness is buried deep inside her mind and I'm not sure how to get her out. I was hoping you could help."

"They did what?" he said, his voice hardening.

"They made me do things I couldn't control," Andi said, her voice starting to shake. "Horrible things I did to my friends and to you."

"I apologize on behalf of my kind," the Spokesman said. "The invasion and trapping you within your consciousness is unforgivable. We have only used that in extreme cases and never to control someone."

"Can you help her?" I asked.

"Yes, although I am not at full strength."

"I can sense your strength," I said. "Even weakened you're bleeding out power."

"As you used all three of us to get here, I will need your help. Keep us joined and I may be able to feed off your energy and the Oracle's."

"What are we going to do?" I asked.

"We're simply going to guide her out. They created a shell around her, a deeper consciousness to keep her confined without control. Then they took over the outer mind, making her bend to their will."

"Can we break it?"

"Yes, of course. It was created by a Council Member and as we are all Dommerian, it can be broken by one as well. Andi, be prepared. It will not hurt your outer body, but will strain your mind so much that it will mimic physical pain."

"Drain my brain, Red," Andi said. "I need to get out and hit something. I hope Cal is nearby."

"Let us begin. Join us more tightly together, Grey."

I took our energy and closed my eyes and imagined pulling us from three balls of energy into one mass. I felt another big surge of power the more I concentrated and our essences moved closer to each other.

A big piece of us stretched out and surrounded Andi, gently spinning around her like an electric windstorm. I felt us pull her gently and then jarred her closer. We started to fly backward and away from where Andi had been, pulling her along.

We backed out and then saw the energy and space between her and her mind pull away. We kept going and then I felt something pop like we had entered a new place.

Then all I sensed was a bright light expanding. Andi burst into a blinding wave of light that covered my sight and surrounded us all. I sucked in air as I felt like I couldn't breathe, then opened my eyes to see myself standing, still holding the hands of the Spokesman and the Oracle.

I let go of their hands and stood by Andi's body. Cal joined me on the other side of her. She took in a deep breath and then exhaled quickly. Her eyes fluttered and then gently opened. She looked at me and said, "Hey, Grey."

"Andi, is it you? I mean totally you?"

She lifted her hand and reached out for mine. As I moved to grab it she turned and punched Cal in the arm.

"Hey!" he said. "What was that for?"

"For not coming with them to get me!"

Cal opened his mouth, but no words came out. She smiled.

It was definitely Andi. She sat up and I wrapped my arms around her. She tried to hug me back but realized she couldn't move her legs.

"Leo, can you reverse that suppressor thing so she can get up?"

"Suppressor?" Andi asked.

"Just a precaution," Leo said. "They were against it."

He pulled out a small tube of liquid and poured it across Andi's legs. She eased herself off the table and stood up.

"I'm so glad you're back," I whispered.

"Me, too," she said as she hugged me tightly. "And I'm sorry."

She eased out of my embrace and looked around at us. "I'm sorry to all of you."

"No," I said. "It wasn't you. I have to admit I was destroyed when I first realized you had turned on us. After the initial shock, we all realized you wouldn't do this on your own. It's just that, you are my closest friend here and we've been on this road together since the first few moments we got here. With everything going on, I just couldn't believe it."

"It's okay Grey," she said. "Thank you all for believing in me, but Grey, you were right to be upset. You've done everything to make us all stronger as a team, and to see what I did without knowing more, I would have probably hunted you down to beat some sense into you. I get it. Thanks for saving me."

I nodded. "We're bringing you back in time to fight a war. You may have been safer here on the table healing."

"Then I would have been pretty ticked I missed the fight," she said. "After what they did and made me do, it's time for payback. You can't imagine what it was like. Sometimes I could see what I was doing and had no control. Other times I was buried deep and just felt like I was nowhere. I was scared I'd never see any of you again."

"We'll need each other," I said. "This one's big and we don't have much time. We're going to take the attack to them on their turf. We need the Councilmen to heal as much as possible for us to have a chance, but I also knew we couldn't do this without you. We're hurting, but we're stronger now that you're back. Are you ready?"

"Just tell me when and where. I need a good fight."

CHAPTER 14:
REUNIFICATION

I felt a sense of relief hearing Andi's words. It was like a broken piece of me had been restored.

"You're definitely our Andi," I said. "The fight will happen soon enough. We'd like to have everyone healed, but we may not have enough time. We'll settle for able right now."

A hand grabbed my shoulder from behind. "We are in," a familiar Councilman said.

I turned. Councilmen Yellow and Purple were sitting up while Red the Spokesman looked on from his bed. He was weak but his eyes were open. It was Purple who had put his hand on me.

The Doctor rushed to the Councilmen and started to examine them.

"We are better, Doctor," the Spokesman said. "Joining with the Oracle and Grey reinvigorated something, and I passed it on to my fellow Councilmen here. There was a new power in that trip."

"That should have weakened you and the Oracle

further," the Doctor said.

He walked over to Councilman Red and did a quick examination. "Your vitals have vastly improved. I agree. Something gave you an increase in power."

"Like jump-starting a dead car battery?" Cal said.

The Doctor blinked and stared for a moment. "Yes, that's a great analogy. Instead of weakening the Spokesman, whatever Grey and the Oracle did actually generated more power, thus jump-starting the Councilman and enhancing his healing process."

"We will be helping in this war," the Spokesman said.

"No," the Doctor argued. "There is no guarantee this will last."

"Doctor, if we do not win this fight, there will be no point. We will be destroyed or locked away somewhere for eons. If I can stand, I will do what I can."

"And I as well," said Councilman Purple.

"This is a battle for the entire Underworld," Councilman Yellow said. "There is nothing more important worth fighting for."

The Doctor shrugged. "Yes, you are all correct. You may not be one hundred percent, but it will take a Dommerian to offset another."

"This is great news," I said. "We need everything we can to even the odds. In fact, we need to get Blue involved. I'm going to go talk to him."

"I'm coming with you," Andi said.

"Maybe you should stay here and rest," I said.

"No, I wanna see Blue. I can help you plan this and will tell you if your ideas are stupid or not."

"She is a blunt one," the Doctor said.

I knew she was right. "We do need all available eyes and ideas. I know you need to rest but time is already against us. Come on."

We entered Blue's tech room. Blue was tinkering on the map. He turned as we walked in and stopped cold when he saw Andi.

"You're back!" he said as he ran to her. As he got closer he moved in for a hug, but then held back and offered a high open palm as a high five instead.

"You can hug me, Brainiac."

He smiled and did.

"How?" he asked.

"I'll explain it later if we survive," I said. "I need to talk to you about something else. I know what you've been doing is important but we're going to need every possible body in this war. We need your abilities, Blue."

He looked down. "I've been thinking about that, but from here I can monitor everything over the mapping and computer systems I've refined. We can use consciousness and mapping to help strategize and catch any surprises."

"He's got a good point," Cal said.

"I know, but we're facing enemies with their own abilities and weaknesses. Blue has a strong elemental gift that we can't afford to leave behind. We need all our strengths."

"Is there anyone else that can help with this?" Andi asked. "What about Leo?"

"No, Leo has the knowledge we need. If we meet someone or something unexpected, he can get that information in a few seconds and that could be critical. We need him ready for that."

I stared at the computer.

"Blue," I said. "Would you consider the connections you have pretty reliable now?"

Blue's head tilted. "Yes, I suppose so. What are you getting at?"

"Kristopher," I said. "We have the ability to reach him

on his computer pretty easily now, right?"

"Yes, that connection is solid. It needed your boost before but now that I have a baseline to follow, we should be good without it."

"Kristopher and I played a lot of strategy video games where we had to command armies against each other. We had to move fast and make quick decisions. He always beat me."

"Being good at a video game doesn't mean he can do that in a real battle," Blue said.

"He's not just good, but one of the top five strategy-based players in the state. Plus, I don't mean he will plan or run the battle, but he knows how to view positions and where things are. Couldn't he do what you do?"

Blue's eyes widened.

"I don't mean as good as you," I said. "Wouldn't you be able to show him everything and what you need him to do? He could monitor it all on his home computer and relay what he sees with a few simple keystrokes. We could then send him questions by simply thinking them."

Blue thought for a moment, then nodded slowly. "Yes, I think it could work. If he can handle it, it wouldn't be hard to show him. I played strategy games, too. Pointing out positions and what the enemy is doing is pretty much what I would be doing. It's not that much different."

"Then let's get him involved now. Need to be sure he's going to be available for the battle, whenever it may happen. I may have to convince him to stay home a couple of days since he's enjoying his summer."

"Then let's not waste any time. You ready?" Blue asked.

I nodded and sat in the nearest chair.

"We need to do this the same way we did before so that if we're on the battlefield, there's no chance of losing the connection."

"Agreed," Blue said. "The channel is ready and I just need to activate it. You should find a dedicated electric field going straight to it. You just need to sense it and jump on it."

Blue reached for his machine. "The channel's open."

I took in a slow breath and let it out, immediately jumping out into the consciousness of the Underworld. The connection upwards to Kristopher's computer was bright and visible. It was glowing and moved like a prism, cutting upwards in different directions. I jumped in, and like a light speed elevator, I felt myself shoot up and was on the other side of Kristopher's computer screen. He wasn't there.

"Kristopher, where are you?" I thought.

I saw the words already formed on his messenger.

Nothing happened for a few seconds, but then words started appearing. "Grey? Is that you?"

"I'm at your machine. Where are you?"

"I'm at the store. Mom sent me to pick some stuff up."

There was a convenience store about four blocks from our houses. I thought of all the times we traveled there on our bikes to run errands for one or both of our mothers.

"You're on your phone?" I asked.

"Yeah, I set up a notification so it dings if I get a message. What's going on?"

"It's important. How soon can you get home?"

"I'm about to pay. I'll be back in a few minutes."

"It's okay. Just stay on your phone. I don't have the time. Look, we're about to go to war. I expect sometime in the next day or two at most. It's critical and we need all hands on deck."

"What do you need from me?"

"I need you to help keep us organized. Blue has parts of the underworld mapped out and he's tagged different types of creatures. He needs to get with you to go over how to work it, so we have your eyes above us. Kind of like the *Empire Overlord* and other war strategy games we used to play."

"The ones you could never beat me at?"

"Yes, those. You won't be building or moving things around, just keeping a bird's-eye view on positions to make sure we're not caught by surprise and keep the line of communication open. The Oracle and I will definitely be able to hear you, but there's a chance we may be able to open the channel so the rest of The Dead Club can, too."

"No way! Like a Supreme General. That would make an awesome game. Underworld War."

"Yes. Blue is too valuable to leave in the war room. We need him out there with us. We may not survive, but we're going to give it all we have."

"Yes, Grey. I know you will."

"Do you have any major plans the next couple of days?"

"Mom wanted to take me out to the pool and do some school shopping. If she does, I'll pull the fever bit."

I laughed. "That still works?"

I remember Kristopher and I dipping our faces in warm water and saying we didn't feel well, usually on a big game release day. A quick check from a Mom's hand would usually get at least one of us a day off of school as long as we didn't overdo it.

"Since you died, I tried it once and Mom didn't even ask if I was faking. I think I can get away with one more if I need to."

"Alright, just try to stay near your computer or your phone."

"It's like we're going to be playing co-op one more time."

"Yeah, but this time if we lose we don't get to start over.

You get me?"

"Yes. It's win or really die."

"More than you know. You can help us win the Underworld. If we lose, I don't know what will happen to me or if I'll ever get to talk to you again, but we have to fight. It won't be easy."

"Then don't lose," Kristopher replied.

"I don't plan to, but we always gotta be ready, right?"

"I didn't forget those two years of scouts."

"We're doing our best to be prepared. Thanks for this."

"The Afterlife is at stake. It's your home now. Nothing to thank me for. You need me, and that's all that needs to be said."

"Thanks, brother. I'll get you hooked up with Blue so you can go over the details."

CHAPTER 15:
PREPARATION

I left the connection and opened my eyes.

"We're good, Blue. You need to give him the quick version of how to do this. How long before you can get him hooked up?"

"The main thing is getting the software on his computer set up with everything he needs. Considering the equipment I'm using down here is ancient by Earth computer standards, it shouldn't take long."

"Then get going, Professor Blue. Kristopher should be back at his machine in a few minutes. We need to start our planning. For now, can you send the coordinates and what you know to the war table?"

Blue nodded and rushed to his computer. I stood up and moved to the table. I sent a mental message out to all.

"We are in the war room. If you are able, please come over now."

Within a few minutes Andi, Cal, Bob, the three other Keepers, and Councilmen Purple and Yellow were around the table.

"The Spokesman required more time," Purple said. "We will be sending him images of what we see."

The Doctor stood off to the side, watching the Councilmen closely. Leo also stood with us while Blue was in mid-conversation with Kristopher. He put on some headphones so they wouldn't interrupt us. I was going to catch him up once we had some kind of plan.

"Where are Grim and the Oracle?" Andi asked.

"We are here," Grim said.

He and the Oracle, who had dark circles around her eyes that made her no less stunning, stood there patiently.

"Everyone contributes," I said. "If something sounds wrong, speak up. Don't keep any opinions to yourself. Everyone here brings some kind of help to the table, but Oracle, you are the one with the most experience. You and the Councilmen."

"Voltaris is mine," Oracle said. "He is the biggest and strongest threat. I took out his kind before."

"But that was with your full-on psychic abilities. You could sense their moves," Grim said. "How will you defeat them without it?"

"Have faith, Grimmy," the Oracle said. "I still had to fight them. Yes, the abilities helped, but I also have rage and vengeance going for me. They've tried to destroy everything we are, and this started with me. It will end with me."

We all paused for a moment.

"You're right, Oracle," I said. "We need to figure out the rest. Who will be the biggest threat besides Voltaris?"

"The other Forta," Oracle said. "If I challenge Voltaris to a one-on-one fight, he can't back down. The others will not interfere so they will work on everyone else. They may not be as strong as Voltaris alone, but together they can devastate us."

"I will take them on," Grim said. "They will be a challenge, even being Death, they are also Underworlders. I have no doubt I could destroy a single Forta but am thirsting to face more. This will be excellent. I haven't had a real combat challenge in so long."

"What about the others?" I asked. "And what can we expect from the Keepers, Bob? Do you think they'll stay neutral?"

"Some turned against me while I was holding off Pink and Green in the Chambers," Grim said.

"We are realm defenders," Bob said. "They shall remain neutral or face me."

"How will the Forta fight you and any Keepers who do join in?" I asked.

"They would recruit Manawa to counteract."

"Manawa? What are they?" Cal asked.

"The Manawa are like us. They break and swarm. Only smaller."

"Most Underworlders just call them Swarmers," Leo said.

"I saw some at my castle," the Oracle said.

"Councilmen," I asked. "I would think you would face Councilmen Pink and Green?"

"Yes, our combined minds can even overpower the Oracle," he said.

"That's never been tested," the Oracle replied sharply. "But I'm sure it would be challenging."

"I say this with no ego," Councilman Purple said, "However, I do believe it to be true. The best we can do is neutralize them. Unless they have learned something new, we are built to be even, no abilities stronger than the other. If the Spokesman is with us, we will outnumber them, but a full defeat is doubtful. If there is a victor, I expect it would take a much longer time than this entire battle will."

"That's okay," Leo said. "In all my studies of war planning, sometimes just keeping a strong foe occupied long enough can help win the overall battle."

"That sounds like it may be our best plan," I said. "I need to know if we all agree. If we defeat what we can and keep the stronger enemies at bay, we may be able to win the main battles."

"So the Forta are the ones we're shooting for and anything else we can't beat fast enough, we keep busy," Cal said.

Grim nodded. "I don't see another course at this time."

"Same here," the Oracle agreed. "We just don't know."

"And they don't expect the Council will be healed or that the Oracle will be there," I said.

"That will help initially," the Oracle said, "But we have to finish it as quickly as possible. The longer it takes, the more we lose that advantage. I believe the biggest battle will be with Voltaris, and if he is able to slow us down, it will give him the upper hand."

We all agreed.

"So that leaves our Dead Club," I said. "Andi and her sticky snot, Cal with his boomerang limbs, Blue with his water and me with my psychic abilities."

"Hey," a voice echoed as Bri appeared. "What about me?"

"Yes, Bri. Was hoping you'd show up."

"I've been saving my energy to appear when I was needed."

I nodded. "Councilmen, Leo couldn't find anything on Brianna's condition. Is there any way you can help her?"

"Let me see," Councilman Yellow said.

He and Purple moved toward Bri, reached out their arms and gently took each of her hands into theirs, holding them for a few moments.

"It is never intended for a soul who has passed on to the next phase from the Underworld to return," Councilman Yellow said. "It is not unheard of, but we have sensed something external has tried to keep you from being fully returned. I expect our Council brothers, the traitors, had a hand in this. We can help some. We cannot fully remove whatever enchantment has been done to you without knowing all the details, which we may not have enough information for, but we can minimize it. Please focus on staying still and here for the next few moments."

Bri squeezed their hands as the Councilmen closed their eyes and their bodies started to emit a soft green glow around them. The glow flowed from their hands through Bri's hands and then their grip broke.

Bri opened her eyes. She had more color to her.

"What happened?" she asked.

"You will be able to stay here in longer waves," Councilmen Yellow said. "We diminished what we could, but that's as much as we can do for now. You will be able to recover faster and maintain more of yourself on this side."

"I can feel a stronger bond to this realm already," Bri said. "There's this constant something trying to pull me back over and over. It's still there, but not as pronounced."

"This helps," I said. "So we can count on Bri with her fire strength a little more. Does anyone know what they may have that our abilities can help with?"

Leo chimed in. "There are many creatures with water and fire-based abilities. Others we simply won't know until we get there."

"So once we get a glimpse of the battlefield we'll have to decide right then and there?"

"Kristopher can help figure that out once the battle starts," Blue said.

We all turned towards him. He had removed his headphones and was facing us.

"Kristopher will be able to quickly assign different colors on his computer screen to enemies with a click of the mouse," Blue said. "We just need to keep the line of communication open and tell him what we see so he can update his aerial-like view of what's going on. I've still got a few more things to show him but he's picking it up quickly. Oh, and one more cool thing that might make it easier."

"What's that?" I asked.

"I am going to be able to translate the messages Kristopher types to be read aloud with his own voice. I was able to get a few vocal samples from him and it may not sound that natural, but it will be easier to hear his voice and not just see what he's typing."

"That's incredible, Blue. You're still finding ways to surprise us."

"This is a big dependency on a connection that is new," Grim said. "How certain are you it will hold?"

Blue nodded. "It will hold. We will be too busy for anyone to pick up on it. That's the plan. The science is good."

"Can you guarantee that?" Grim asked.

"Of course not. Nothing is ever truly guaranteed," Leo replied.

"That's good enough for me," I said. "Blue has been working on this enough and I can jump in that channel without much effort."

"But what if you're in the middle of a fight?" Cal asked.

"I think it'll be fine."

"How?" Cal asked.

"I trust in Blue's network. If it works, we'll know immediately on the battlefield. If not, we'll improvise. It's what we've done since we got here."

"Can't argue with that," Cal agreed.

Blue put his headphones back on and returned to his conversation with my best living friend.

"So this is our plan," I said. "Blue will finish coordinating with Kristopher. This is our starting point. We will provide as many details as we can once we get there. We'll adjust and we will have to rely on Kristopher's guidance. He'll know what to do."

"This appears to be the best starting option against the unknown," Councilman Yellow said.

"Once they are ready and we get to the battlefield, Oracle and Grim will handle Voltaris and the rest of the Forta. Bob expects the Swarmers to be there. Then it's Council against Council. As for the rest of us, if there are elemental beings, we take on the ones that best match our abilities. If not, we identify advantages to take on whatever is out there. We stop and destroy what we can or neutralize. Our main goal is to stop the Forta and Voltaris."

"With the hope that will stop them all," Councilman Purple said.

There were a few nods and I felt the agreement from the Council's thoughts.

"Please," I said. "If anyone has a better option or thinks we need to change something, speak now."

We all looked at each other. No one said a word.

"The fate of the Underworld depends on everyone here and a boy on Earth who knows only some of what we are facing," the Oracle said. "This isn't perfect, but with time against us and the unknown that we simply can't plan for, I agree. We have to go in and as Grey put it, improvise. This ability helped them save us from the threat of Purgatory being destroyed, and they knew so little of what they were facing then. I will fight until I can no longer fight to save our world, even if it is the last thing I ever do."

Everyone nodded.

I think we realized at that moment this could be the last thing any of us might ever do.

CHAPTER 16:
MOTIVATION

We still had logistics to work out. Where we would appear and what positions to take, but none of that could be solid until we were face to face with the enemy. I had one main concern.

"We have to wait until we know where they are or make a move, right?" I asked. "Is there any way we could get any kind of notice? Even if it was just a few seconds? That could buy us enough time to at least get in place before we start to fight. That could be valuable."

"If we knew where they were or their formations, it would be a critical advantage," the Oracle said.

"What about your history, Oracle?" I asked. "Voltaris wants vengeance against you. Think about it. How would he best go about it?"

"He just wants to destroy her, no matter how," Grim said.

"Not necessarily," I said. "Up to this point, everything has been centered around the Oracle. Her past, trying to frame her and drive her nuts, taking her out of the equation. Everything has been about her directly or indirectly."

"I think I understand where you are going, Grey," the Oracle said. "If I were Voltaris, I would want to not only win, but to do it with more than just vengeance. A total, complete defeat, meaning righting the past."

"What are you thinking?" I asked.

"It could be at one of my old homes or favorite locations like the waterfall cave or the Arena just to add to the humiliation if they were to win. It could be at the Citadel where I defeated them. Then again, that might be what they want us to think and set up a trap like they did in Foglia Forest."

"The Council Chambers," Councilman Purple said. "Now that it is abandoned, I can return and use its constant movement to possibly give us a sense of where they may be. They have already proven to be worthy at hiding themselves."

"That sounds like the best option so far," I said. "It gives us some kind of chance. You can probably cover more ground than we could in a short time."

"I agree," the Oracle said.

"Then we have no time to waste," Councilman Purple said. "Councilman Yellow shall remain in case anything befalls me."

"I must reiterate I am against this," the Doctor said.

"You were listening to everything?" Cal asked.

"It is my duty to monitor the Councilmen."

"Then go with him," I said. "If they do sense you there, they will still think you are just treating him."

"He is hurt and I am treating him," the Doctor said.

"Then it all makes sense, Doc," Cal said. "Why are you still here?"

Councilman Purple and the Doctor disappeared.

"I guess now we wait," I said.

Blue was still talking to Kristopher. I walked over.

"How's it going?"

"He picked it up quickly, like you thought," Blue said. "Fortunately I used to play war games like *Empire Overlord*, too. I've been able to get a similar layout. I've given him the full maps, so as long as it's someplace that Leo and I have mapped out, we'll be okay. If it's something new that I don't know about, this may be all for nothing."

"He's pretty quick at improvising. Can I talk to him again or do you need more time?" I said.

"Just make it fast. Still a few things I'd like to double-check."

I pulled into the channel and appeared on Kristopher's computer.

"You getting it?" I asked.

"Yes," he typed, and this time I could hear his voice as the words appeared in my head. "It was confusing at first, but you were right. That Blue is brilliant. I can quickly label people, or creatures, or whatever might appear. If something unexpected comes up, I can use similar builds to create a hill or building as you tell me. I think I'm good to go."

"It's really nice to hear your voice again. Even if you sound a little like a droid. We were just discussing that there is a small chance we might arrive somewhere you don't have a map for. How fast do you think you can adjust to that?"

"I'll just pull up any random map if I have to. Won't be the best option, but once I get every item and body positioned, it will be easy."

"Okay, so you're good, then. No interruptions anytime soon?"

"Should be fine. My Mom is out for the rest of the day.

I convinced her to go see my Aunt Hilda. She doesn't leave me alone much since you've been gone, but I told her I had a summer essay to write if I wanted to get into the advanced English class this year."

"Advanced English?" I thought. "You complained when you had to read one book in fifth grade."

"I wasn't serious!" Kristopher typed. "I wanted some free time. I laid the guilt on thick. You would have been proud."

I laughed out loud. For a second I thought of how many times he'd done that to his Mom. Yeah, it was a lousy thing to do, but it didn't make it any less funny.

"Okay, Kristopher. Thank you again. You're helping save the Underworld."

"I'm not just doing this for you now," Kristopher said. "I've been thinking a ton about this and realize it's also my future. The future of everyone here. One day it'll be our time and we need to have a place to go. If it's run by evil, what chance do our souls have of moving on to paradise or where we deserve to be? It's bigger than me and bigger than you. It makes me want to puke just thinking about it. Feels like when we rode on the roller coaster that had the triple loop."

I knew what he meant.

"Okay, Kristopher, hopefully the next time I talk to you it'll be during our battle. Eat something so you won't pass out."

"I'll be ready, Grey."

I broke the connection.

I opened my eyes and looked at Blue. "Just let me know when you're comfortable. Hopefully we'll hear back from Purple soon."

Before I finished my next breath, the Councilman appeared with the Doctor beside him.

We all turned toward them.

"So?" the Oracle asked.

"We took the Council Chambers traveling through enough of the Underworld that we would have located them. However it was the same signal everywhere. They must have done something to mass produce that signal so it cannot be tracked."

"Like they're jamming it?" Blue asked.

"I suppose so."

"So no element of surprise on our side," Cal said. "They'll have that advantage if they appear at any time."

I felt a static buzz in my head.

"No need," the Oracle said.

Her eyes were wide and she was staring off into nothing.

"What do you mean?" Councilman Purple asked.

"They've just contacted me."

I heard every word, though it was still filled with static. The signal must have been meant only for the Oracle, but I was close enough that I was able to hear it, too.

"Voltaris just popped into my head. He made his signal clear. We will meet at the Citadel in one hour. He wants his victory to be pure for the history books and wants no doubts or excuses when it's over."

"That's a pretty big thing to say when he already tried to take so many of us out of the equation," Andi said.

"I don't know if that will matter," the Oracle said.

"Why?" Andi asked.

"He wants to face me directly. No matter what happens in this battle, I'm the one he wants to defeat in a one-on-one fight. I think even if we were to win this war, he would still be happy as long as he defeats me."

The room was silent.

"Now we know the time and the place," I said. "If we are to take Voltaris at his word, there should be no surprise attack."

"We still don't know how big their numbers are or what exactly we're facing," Cal said.

"No, but this still helps," Blue said. "Unless he's lying about the location, we should be able to arrive on the grounds with enough time to evaluate and get our information to Kristopher."

"That's something, I guess," Cal said. "We'll still be outnumbered."

"You are all more powerful than you realize," the Oracle said. "Along with me, Grim, the Keepers and the Council, you are all formidable opponents. Trust in your abilities. They've served you well so far."

I felt a little better hearing this, but the unknown was still there. I wasn't sure if we could trust Voltaris, but what he said made sense. He fully expected to win and didn't want anyone he would rule in the Underworld to doubt his victory. There were small details like trying to weaken the Oracle and getting rid of so many others, but once the battle was over, all that would be remembered is how it ended, and he knew it. We had to do to him what he wanted to do to Oracle. We not only had to defeat him, but we had to do it soundly. Our plan had too many unknowns, but we also had some of the oldest, wisest and most powerful creatures in our corner. That was something I couldn't ignore.

"We have an hour," I said. "We are all ready to go and we have a plan. Let's decide on who will appear where to begin with, even though I expect that will change. Oracle, please tell us the details about the Citadel. We already saw its medieval castle layout, but there are grounds in front of it and within the castle itself. We need to be ready for everything."

The Oracle nodded. "Blue, please pull up the castle

specs."

The table in front of us was filled with a map of the castle and the surrounding area. She pointed to the outer parts.

"Nothing special about the grounds here. There are some trees between the structure you visited and the bridge where you found my broken heel. As for the castle grounds, the inner area is actually a better option for us since there are many places to cover. There are three major levels, a guard tower in each of the three corners still standing and the dining and main meeting rooms. The center of the castle is mainly one large square of land that was primarily used for battle training. With so many options, we could fight in different areas if necessary."

"What about behind the castle?" I asked.

"That's primarily trees and marsh. The inner castle and front area are the only open parts. The open center area is the most logical battle area. That field is still flat and not many places to hide or to gain a higher ground advantage. Unless they want a melee mass attack."

She reached down to the map and spread some of the screen by the castle. She pointed toward the front gate.

"The large hallway you entered before, that is larger than my main castle room, but would make for an awkward space to fight. They may have fighters on the upper floors if they have any kind of weapons, but for the most part creatures prefer hand-to-hand."

I nodded. "So if we appear in the flat entrance before the bridge, that should buy us time?"

"Yes, I would think so."

"What if they've blocked communications?" Andi asked. "Like at the Council Chambers?"

Councilman Yellow shook his head. "Unless they know about the new connections you have established, that is highly doubtful. Not only is this a difficult thing to accomplish but they would block their own communications in the process."

"Then let's hope that's what they do," I said. "Blue, please contact Kristopher to be ready in an hour and to pull up the Citadel map. It's time."

Blue nodded and moved to his computer to make the call. I kept staring at the map.

"So, this is it?" I asked.

"It appears so," Grim said. "We must all be ready."

"I am ready," a loud voice boomed. The Spokesman entered the room, his red collar glowing brightly.

The Doctor shook his head.

"Good to see you, Councilman," I said.

He nodded back.

I looked at my friends Andi, Cal, Blue and Bri.

"We can't predict what will happen, but just like we have always done since we got here, we'll figure it out. We'll arrive together and separate as needed. We won't have much time. A few minutes at most as we near the castle. Are we all in?"

"You know I am," Andi said. Her eyes watered and turned red. "I owe them."

"They messed with one of us," Cal said. "That means they messed with all of us. They can't take over."

Bri appeared. "I know I was never a big fighter and scared of my own shadow once, but I know what's at stake. I'll be strong."

"You are strong," I said.

She was stronger than she knew. According to Grim, we all were. I just hoped that he was right.

"Leo, you'll be able to help run things here?"

"It would be best. I'll have my books at the ready and will feed Kristopher any weaknesses and a list of creatures to pass on to you."

"That works. Anyone have anything else to add?"

No one replied. We were done and just had to wait for our battle.

The next thirty minutes moved slowly. Cal practiced throwing his limbs around while Andi and Blue traded snot and water attacks against a wall. Bri worked on holding her form as long as she could. She was able to maintain her presence between 2 to 3 minutes before losing herself and was able to reappear within twenty seconds. She also sustained longer streams of fire. Considering she had no control previously, it was a major improvement.

Grim walked into the room where we were warming up.

"It's almost time," he said. "You all know what's at stake. Whatever happens, know that I'm proud of all of you. You've brought new life into this Underworld. Even with all that has happened, you are still here. Still together. I've never had a reason to be a part of a team. My job is pretty lonely and I only interact with my Reapers, which are still just an extension of me."

"You going soft on us, Grim?" Cal said.

Grim's eyes locked on him.

"Let him finish," I said.

I knew it wasn't easy for him to open up.

"Sorry," Cal said. "You've been a great guide under all that death stuff."

Grim's face softened.

"You've all helped me find some of what I used to be. I am starting to understand the Oracle and I had not made new friends in several centuries before you showed up. Grey was the one who helped me see at first, but you have all become a part of the Underworld and have all made my job more enjoyable. And I enjoy my job immensely. If we survive this, it will be because of your efforts and your human stubbornness, which you haven't lost in death."

I smiled. "Thank you for saying so, Grim. I hope we do survive to enjoy the rest of our eternity."

"Then let's go. No more time to waste. Forever is a long time. Let's hope we have the luxury of enjoying it."

CHAPTER 17:
PARLEY INTEL

We appeared in the open field. No one was around, so it didn't look like a sneak attack, but we were careful. I didn't sense any danger, but they had hidden it well before.

I immediately jumped up to test the connection with Kristopher. I didn't get a lock right away and felt a little anxious. I couldn't see the connection and looked around several times before realizing it was where it had always been. I had too much going on in my head. I easily jumped up and Kristopher was there.

"Good?" I asked.

"Good," he typed.

I went back down and opened my eyes. I thought up towards Kristopher while looking at my dozen companions.

"I'm on the ground now. Can you still get me?"

"Loud and clear," I heard his voice say as he typed.

I nodded to the group. Our Dead Club, Grim, the Oracle, the three Underworld Councilmen and four

Keepers. Fourteen. I started to feel something in the pit of my stomach, but Oracle started walking and I forgot about it as I caught up.

We were spaced out a few steps from each other and headed across the field towards the bridge and the line of trees that separated it from the Citadel that we still couldn't see. I imagined a huge army waiting just past the trees to pounce on us. We needed enough time to at least make it to the castle to have any chance of getting our plan together.

We reached the bridge and thinned our ranks as we crossed, led by the Oracle and Grim. We passed through the trees and I looked up, expecting to see something hiding in the branches.

Nothing.

The Citadel came into view. It seemed bigger than when we first saw it. Then again, everything seemed bigger now. We had so much on the line and I could feel the tension inside me. It was like when Kristopher and I sat on the Scream ride at an amusement park for the first time. We were held down tight in our seats and had no idea exactly when they would push the button to send us shooting straight up 20 stories high. I felt that same anticipation of waiting to be launched into the air and seeing the entire park from its highest point within seconds.

I hadn't felt anything even close to this kind of anxiety since the first time we fought and lost against Craver & Conniver, which seemed like a lifetime ago.

We moved toward the castle. The front gate was open. I saw some heads from the upper floors looking down.

"There will be a parley in the main chambers as you enter," one of the heads said.

"Parley?" Andi asked.

"A pre-battle meeting," Grim said. "Usually to discuss

any details."

The creature that had given us the parley message had walked out far enough for me to realize it wasn't something I had seen before. It had a tiny nose and rectangular eyes and a couple of long claws.

"Jaggers," the Oracle said.

I sent a message to Kristopher that there were at least two of them. After about ten more steps, he replied.

"Leo says Jaggers are small but vicious fighters. They mainly use their teeth and claws."

We walked through and as we entered the main hallway, Voltaris stood there with three more Forta around him. They were in a semi-circle, waiting for us. I quickly sent the mental message to Kristopher on what I was seeing and the Forta's positions in the room. I checked the faces around me and no one seemed to either notice or care what I was doing.

"They aren't in any formation yet," I said. "They're just waiting."

"Waiting for what?" Kristopher replied.

"We're about to find out."

The Oracle, Grim and our three Councilmen stopped a few steps in front of Voltaris. I didn't see the traitor Councilmen Pink and Green.

"I am surprised you are here," Voltaris said. "I almost believed you would not show and we would have to hunt you down."

"Did you think we wouldn't, knowing what's at risk?" the Oracle said.

"You aren't at full capacity," Voltaris sneered. "I thought your boyfriend would be here to fight in your place."

Grim clenched his bony fists. "You underestimate her strength. She no more needs me to fight her battles than you need an ego boost. I have no doubt she will defeat you."

"I'll be happy to disappoint Death. When all is said and done, I may even let you keep your job."

"Are you gonna keep talking smack or are we gonna do this?" Andi yelled.

Voltaris turned toward her. "You even brought these insignificant ones? You must be desperate. My battle is with the Oracle. Whatever else happens is of minor consequence. You are not only outnumbered but you risk losing your entire party. I will make an offer."

"What offer is that?" the Oracle said.

"If you give up now, I will not immediately destroy these others. I will enslave them, of course, but I will spare their souls."

The Oracle looked back at us. I could see her contemplating.

"Don't even think about it," I said.

"Yeah, we didn't come here just to look cool," Cal said. "We're here to finish this."

The Oracle smiled and looked at each of us for a moment. Her face turned serious before turning back to the Forta leader.

"You have your answer," she said.

Voltaris smiled. "Then there will be no mercy."

The Oracle stared hard into his eyes. "I wasn't planning on giving you any."

"My only interest is in your complete and total defeat. Shall we proceed to the central grounds?"

He motioned past the hallway into the open center of the Citadel and started walking.

The Oracle followed and we moved behind her. As we came into the clearing, there were more enemies. There were three Jaggers, including the one that had met us at the gate, and I noticed a mass of smaller creatures surrounding the outer parts. I couldn't see them clearly but they all held swords.

"The creatures I see the most are these small, stocky ones hanging back on the battlegrounds. Any ideas?"

Kristopher didn't answer right away.

"Are they using swords?" Kristopher asked.

"Yes, all of them."

"Leo says those are Grountees. Small and tough. Easy to defeat one on one and not great swordsmen even though that's their weapon of choice. However, there are so many they can overwhelm an enemy with their sheer numbers. He said the Underworld commonly refers to them as Grunts."

Grunts. These Grunts appeared to have surrounded the entire area. They were the most of any being I was able to see. At least thirty or forty of them and I'm sure there were more behind them.

I glanced at the other creatures and a few looked a lot more dangerous than the Grunts or Jaggers.

One was a yellow female, with what looked like wings of liquid. Near her was a demonic looking creature, with short horns. It looked like a more sinister gargoyle with an opening in its throat the shape of a pear. I quickly sent these images to Kristopher and the placement of where this battle would begin. I wasn't sure if the Oracle and Voltaris would battle one-on-one while we all watched or if it would be an open fight. We'd all find out soon enough.

Kristopher responded quickly. "Leo says the horned one is a common demon and will have heat and fire similar to Bri. The female is a Flamorda. She is water-based and can fly. Both are dangerous as expected."

"I think everything in this place is dangerous," I thought back to him.

We moved closer to the center and I kept my eyes open. Something gleamed to my right. There were two large, wooden racks, holding various weapons. I was able to make out some swords, a couple of staffs and an axe from my quick glance. We kept moving.

Everyone was concentrating on Voltaris and the Oracle as we neared the center. I decided to try my expansion plan.

I stopped a moment and took in a breath. I looked at my companions and opened my mind, but not directly to them, as that would be expected. Instead, I took my energy up into the cloud and shot it back down to them like I was bouncing off a satellite.

I hit my team with one word.

"Acknowledge."

Blue and Cal turned toward me before looking back. Andi kept her cool and slowly nodded. Bri disappeared for a moment and reappeared holding a thumbs up. I didn't try to signal the Oracle since she was already weak. I didn't want to give her more to worry about. Grim simply answered me back, already able to jump on the signal and return it instead of coming back to me directly. His message was simple.

"We are good."

I relayed the information on the creatures I'd seen so far to the team and told them to try and let me know what they saw. As we moved closer more creatures encircled us. Councilmen Pink and Green were waiting in the center. They locked onto Councilmen Red, Purple and Yellow and never shifted their focus. There was no doubt they would be battling each other.

Behind them I saw different creatures. One was white and had thin, almost web-like skin that opened and closed as if the wind were thrashing it around. It expanded its arms and had webbing around its limbs then looked like it was carried into the air, flying in a small circular formation. Behind that was an orange, four-armed being with thin tentacles for fingers that were constantly moving. The tentacles and parts of its chest looked more metallic and as smooth as chrome. It had long lips, no nose, and two round, yellow eyes. I took them all in and sent the images to my team and Kristopher.

"Leo's results," Kristopher said. "The orange thing is a Manet and is metal-based. It uses electricity for its protection and can release charged metal fragments from its tentacles. The one with the spider skin that shifts with the air is wind-based. It's manipulating the air around it and is taking a battle stance when it flexes its body to distract as it attacks. It's called an Olarnea."

I saw one more thing I didn't recognize. It was a ball floating in the air. It was smooth and a marble black and gold mix. It was hard to see and seemed to be vibrating.

"I'm not sure what I'm looking at," I told Kristopher as I described it to him.

"No need," Bob the Keeper said in our heads. "These are Manawa. The Swarmers. Expected counter to us. That is a natural state you see. When they break into smaller pieces, will outnumber us. It will be a challenge with our four. One I am happy to accept."

Flamorda, Manet, a demon and Olarnea. I was never going to remember all that.

"Let's make this simple," I said to everyone. "They are elemental like we are. Let's just call them something easier like Swarmers instead of Manawa. How about Firedemon, Watergirl, Metallic Squid and Windspider?"

My years of reading comic books were finally paying off.

"Thanks, Grey," Cal said, sounding relieved. "I was trying to figure out how to spell their names in my head and started thinking about pitches instead."

"Things are complicated enough," Andi said.

I continued. "Trying to counter each of our strengths makes sense. Do you have their placements now?"

"Yes," Kristopher added. "Is the plan to go with or against their matches? Leo says matching up with element against element, or as close as possible, would be the best way to begin to get a measure of abilities and see what you're up against. If you are strong enough to cancel each other out, it may buy time."

I agreed for now. We didn't know much.

"So Bri and Blue vs Firedemon and Watergirl," I said in everyone's heads. "Cal, you should be better matched with the Metallic Squid and Andi maybe you can snot up that Windspider's wings."

Kristopher broke back in. "Once the Oracle and Voltaris battle begins, Leo says to move quickly to your respective positions. The fire and water elements are on the first side you entered and the others are on the farther end behind the Council members. Allow the Council members to engage against each other."

Things were working, but moving fast. Voltaris finally stopped almost dead center of the open battleground.

The Oracle stopped and raised her palms toward us. We all stepped back except for Grim. He never lost his focus on Voltaris.

"You know you need to step back, Grimmy," the Oracle said without feeling.

"Yes, Grim One," Voltaris said. "Step back as the lady commands you. Watch her die helplessly."

Grim let out a half-smile. "I'll remember those words when you fall."

"Without her psychic abilities, this will not last long. You may not even need to fight as this may be over before you even get to engage."

The Oracle moved. She ran right at him and Voltaris wasn't expecting it. Still, he dodged easily and reached out a hand, knocking her to the ground. Voltaris sneered towards Grim as she fell.

"Are you ready to run in and save her?" he asked.

Two Forta I hadn't seen before moved behind Voltaris and the three Jaggers stood at attention behind them, as if expecting Grim to strike.

Grim crossed his arms and watched.

The Oracle spun while still on her back and kicked Voltaris on the side of his leg, knocking him to his knees. He turned to look at her as she struck him across the face twice in a blur of fists. He moved back.

"We shall have a battle after all," he growled.

Grim flew in a blur and struck down all three Jaggers at once, bringing them down easily before attacking the two Forta.

The battle was officially on.

CHAPTER 18:
UNDERWORLD WAR

I saw Grim quickly take down the Forta, but unlike the Jaggers, they jumped right back up and were coming at him at the same time. As he easily dodged them, the three Forta who had stood with Voltaris at the parley appeared and ran straight towards him. They planned to keep him busy. Even Death had to figure out a strategy.

Before they reached him I sent out a quick mental shout out. "Move!"

Bri and Blue rushed behind us toward Firedemon and Watergirl and I rushed with Cal and Andi towards the others. As I moved, the four Keepers buzzed past me. The Swarmer with the marble looking body exploded into smaller flying creatures, looking like a mass of tiny fairies. They were definitely smaller than what Bob broke down to and they spun around the four Keepers. I turned back towards Metallic Squid and Windspider with Cal a step ahead of me as usual. Andi shot some snot balls toward Windspider but it moved quickly around and started flapping its wings and using its wind wake to toss rocks and debris at her. Andi was quick, though, and easily dodged them.

It looked like this would be a tough battle. Cal was in step with me and moved toward Metallic Squid. I was the odd one out but quickly focused my mind on the enemies that Cal and Andi were facing. I was able to mentally buzz around their heads and each turned as I tapped to a different part of their minds. Andi and Cal rushed in. I wanted to know how Blue and Bri were doing and no sooner had I thought it when I saw their enemies in front of me. I stopped for a moment and realized that I was looking through Bri and Blue's eyes almost at the exact same time. I was on the psychic connection but by thinking about what I wanted to see, instead of just an audio connection, I was inside their heads. I couldn't control them, but I was there. It was like when I had allowed Grim to possess me once. They were still in control and I was just riding along.

Bri was popping in and out with fireballs against the Firedemon and Blue and the flying Watergirl were trading water. Blue threw his water balls while Watergirl shot fast streams from her wings and mouth at Blue. They were all hitting each other here and there but mostly their water and fire would cancel out and die somewhere in the middle, doing nothing. Bri had a slight advantage by being able to disappear, so she was landing more hits but they didn't seem to faze the demon. I then thought about Andi and Blue and I felt a jolt as I could now see all four of my friends' perspectives. It was harder to concentrate. I couldn't imagine how Grim did this with all his reapers.

I glanced over at Grim. He was hard to see as he and the Forta moved almost as fast as wind. He was facing all five Forta and was able to knock them back easily, but they were strong. They'd get back up and start over. Then I heard a voice yell. Then another.

The Grunts.

They had remained on the outer rim of the fight but were being called into action. As they moved closer, I got a better look. They were about four feet tall and had small black circles for eyes. More began to yell. With their mouths open I saw that they had upper fangs that extended down to their chins and flat ears that pointed sideways. Their yellow skin was mostly hairless. They descended towards us.

Kristopher broke in. "Grey, incoming. That first wave of Grunts appears to be heading towards Grim."

The tracking was working.

After the first batch of Grunts moved, more joined in, running towards the other fights. There were more than forty or fifty of them and they were coming from everywhere. A group broke off and moved toward Andi and Cal. The first few reached Grim and started attacking with thin swords.

The Grunts distracted Grim briefly, but he was able to fend them off while keeping the Forta back. Then more Grunts reached him. I moved forward and without thinking I pictured pushing them back and the Grunts fighting Grim flew in the air and dropped their swords. I felt them. As more attacked, I did the same. I could feel my mental energy pushing back the hordes. Grim grabbed a few and flung them into a castle column hard enough that their heads cracked and they fell in small heaps. I put more force into my thoughts and threw back several at a time.

"Grey, over here!" Cal yelled.

About a dozen Grunts were now surrounding him and Andi. I flipped into their heads. They were both keeping Windspider and Metallic Squid at bay, but once the Grunts arrived, they each got hit after backing away to avoid their swords. Andi was using snot shots but there were too many and a few got through her attack. I ran to them to try and help. My head was shooting everywhere. I flipped back from Grim to Andi and Cal while popping in and out of Blue and Bri's heads, too. No Grunts on their end yet but they weren't making much progress. They were surviving but still mostly neutralizing their enemies instead of getting or inflicting pain.

I felt my fists tighten as I concentrated and was able to flip back seven or eight Grunts at a time. I made their swords fly out of their hands. I looked back and Grim was easily throwing more aside and with much more force than I was as he tried to keep his mind on the Forta. More rushed at us. Now it looked like all the Grunts were coming, the larger batch heading towards me, Andi and Cal. A few more were still coming at Grim.

A loud roar came up and Grim threw out a banshee scream, striking all the Grunts near him and one of the Forta that had fallen with a dark cloud of energy that split the Grunts apart. Their bodies broke in half and a blue mist rose. He had separated their souls. The Forta was still down and didn't split in two, but was staggering and struggling to get up. Grim went back to the remaining Forta and it came at him with everything it had. I could sense that attack had weakened Grim a little.

I flipped back and took an extra few seconds to try and gather my strength. I felt my power surging but held on, letting it grow. It was pulsing in my head, ready to release but I held it a little longer. As we were smothered by more Grunts, I felt the tip of a spear graze my chest and just before it entered I let go.

There was a small boom as they all flew back, even two of the Forta near Grim were drawn off their feet and to the ground. The Grunts were gone. Some split in half, releasing their souls and others were just unconscious, as far as I could tell. I didn't know I had that kind of power.

Then a metal sound echoed loudly enough to make me and those around me cringe. We all stopped fighting and turned toward the sound.

The Oracle and Voltaris were in the center. Voltaris had just slammed two long axes against each other, which had caused the huge sound. We figured this out in the next few seconds as he clanged them again. The Oracle had no weapon but stood her ground, unfazed by the loud boom. I looked back and no one else was fighting. The entire remaining sides were watching the events in the center, and then I felt a burst of energy from the weapon racks I had seen earlier and a strong pull on an object in the midst of them. It was the Oracle. She had locked onto a weapon and then she flung it across the field. The Oracle didn't look up as the shining object reached her. She simply raised a hand and caught it.

The straight-bladed Broadsword she had chosen looked like it was made for her. She held it and spun it and as Voltaris came down with one of his axes, she deflected it with another loud clang and sidestepped, then swung her sword back at him. As he tried to pull his axe up, she moved closer and punched him in the jaw.

He fell back but stayed on one knee. One axe fell to the ground as he grabbed his jaw. The Oracle moved up and he struck her in the ribs with a backhand that sounded like a tractor hitting a tree.

She jumped back and winced.

Voltaris stood up and extended his arms out.

"I wanted all of you to stop fighting to witness this battle. The Oracle may not be as weak as I thought, but she will only delay the inevitable. Once I defeat her the rest of my army will destroy you all. Now, bear witness."

He stood back up, but the Oracle didn't wait. She sliced her sword and he eased his head back. The blade's tip scratched across Voltaris' chest and cut some of the material he was wearing, but didn't break the skin. Voltaris came back at her and swung his single axe. Their weapons clashed and went into a frenzied exchange of swings, parries and dodges.

"What's going on?" Kristopher asked.

I had gotten lost in the battle.

"The Oracle and Voltaris, the Forta leader, are going at it with axes and a sword. It's a great fight."

"Grey, remember that marathon game we played that one day we skipped school when *Empire Overlord II* came out? We went up against those players from New York and we had them, but what happened in the end?"

I remembered that. We went almost ten straight hours and had the game won, but our opponents had launched side Artificial Intelligence battles as we moved for our final strike. We went for the kill and attacked the main two opponents. We had them beat, but we ignored the side battles. The AI armies the other team had defeated then became part of their army, more than doubling their ranks. Just when we had their power down to almost nothing, the new AI armies joined in and the extra soldiers and firepower it gave them destroyed our advantage in less than a minute.

I was ignoring what was around me.

"I get you, Kristopher. Everyone else is just staring."

"Nothing's been happening," Kristopher said. "If the Oracle loses, you'll have no chance. If she wins, you may not, either. There are still five more of the Forta."

We had been at a stalemate the entire time. Each of us was holding our own, even with almost all the Grunts gone or defeated, but it wouldn't take much to sway it one way or the other. We had fire against fire, water against water and electricity and wind against snot and flying arms. Even though Grim was winning, just as he'd take something down, he had to block out the others. The Councilmen were simply staring at each other, concentrating so hard with neither side having a clear advantage or harming each other in any way.

Something had to change. I jumped through the consciousness of my fellow Clubbers. They were tired and were consumed by the fight before them.

"Switch," I said in their heads.

I felt them get startled. They started to look at me.

"Don't turn!" I yelled in their heads. "Keep watching the Oracle fight, but listen. We're getting nowhere. It may change over time but right now they're simply weakening us. Our opponents aren't stronger, but the problem is we aren't, either. It may not make sense but be ready to move towards another enemy. If there are any weak spots, then we eliminate what we can, take any possible advantage, then move on to help each other. Is everyone clear? Don't nod. Just call out in your heads."

"I understand" and "Yeses" echoed in my head.

"Don't take your eyes off the fight, but shift your steps as if you're just trying to get a better view. Slowly."

I felt their anticipation as they waited for my instructions.

"Andi, go to Bri's Firedemon. Bri, take on Blue's Watergirl. Let's see if your fire can beat her water. Blue, move to the Metallic Squid Cal was taking on and Cal, go to the Windspider. We'll switch again if we have to, but we should confuse them at first. I'll try to jump in and out. If we are able to take one down, then move on to help someone else. See if you find a pattern or weak spot. Kristopher and Leo, let us know if you have any ideas. I'm going to open the channel to spread Kristopher's voice to all of us if he's able to help."

I moved around as others were cheering on or simply watching the Oracle and Voltaris' grand battle, which was continuing and getting better with each strike.

Everyone gasped as Voltaris grabbed Oracle by the back of the neck and slammed her into the ground. They gasped again as she jumped right up, spit out the dirt and blood in her mouth and yelled defiantly. She swung her sword and as Voltaris backed away, she slid down and kicked him on a shin, bringing him down.

We were all able to shift slow enough that no one paid attention. We were in different places, but near our new enemies. We would be ready once this battle was over. Right now, it was the Oracle's show. I wanted to will her to win but knew I couldn't interfere. She would never forgive me if it weren't a fair fight.

The Oracle and Voltaris exchanged blows with their weapons, but couldn't hit each other. I could still sense the dullness of the Oracle's powers. She couldn't use them to sense his movements. My abilities weren't strong enough to do that, but not having that must have felt strange to her. I held back my desire to jump into her head. She would notice it and it could distract her. This was a street fight to the death. Voltaris was overconfident and thought it would be over quickly, but they were already long past a fast resolution.

The Oracle broke into a run and stuck her sword into the ground and threw herself airborne. Voltaris looked up, not expecting this but threw his axe across his face as her feet were about to strike him and he knocked her legs sideways. He brought his free hand down and she flew hard into the ground. He smiled as she lay there. He could have struck but took a moment.

I felt true fear for the first time since the battle started. I jumped mentally to the weapons cache and boosted several swords and flail, a shaft with a spiked ball on the end, and was ready to throw them towards Voltaris. I heard a low grunt. I turned and saw Grim raising his arms, about to head forward.

A sharp burst of energy filled my mind as the Oracle's head turned around.

"No!" she screamed in my head and Grim's.

She jumped up and was breathing heavily, stepping back as Voltaris laughed.

"Do not interfere," her voice boomed in our heads. "No matter what happens. One of us has to win this without help. Even if it means my life, you cannot interfere or the future leadership could be in question. History will be marred. Those are my wishes and they will be respected. Am I clear?"

Grim stepped back and I let the weapons fall. We knew she was right.

Her sword was still in the ground and Voltaris picked up his second axe. He raised his arms and held the pair over his head. "Not having the advantage of knowing my next move isn't so easy, is it Oracle? You have been a worthy opponent, but that ends now."

He ran at her with full speed in a hulking dash of movement. He swung both axes, one sideways and one downward, leaving her little room to move. The Oracle then threw herself forward, getting horizontal and forming a spear with her body. She twisted as the axes came at her from the side and above and slammed into his chest as the top axe drove into her body. She struck him first but with less than a second difference the axe blade buried deep into her shoulder before flying back out, taking a chunk of her flesh with it.

Voltaris flew backward, dropping his axes as he landed. His momentum was so fast that the counterstrike knocked him back just as hard as his attack. He was on his back and tried to get up, but was dazed.

The Oracle was on the ground and also tried to get up, but staggered. She instead crawled like a crab toward her sword and pulled on its handle to get herself on her feet. She held herself up and her legs were shaking as she tried to gather herself. Voltaris was turned on his side trying to drive himself up.

The Oracle stared at her enemy and didn't hesitate. She moved forward, stepping slowly at first, then broke into a trot, weaving to her left and right. Voltaris saw her and got to his knees, trying to pull himself up. Her pace picked up as he got to his feet and she suddenly yelled in defiance. He grabbed an axe and raised an arm to strike but then moved the axe across his torso to block her attack once he realized she would get to him first. Her sword came down, but instead of a big clang of weapons towards his chest, the Oracle drove the sword straight through his foot. It pierced completely through with only the handle sticking up over the top of his boot and he dropped his axe. He yelled in pain and she went into a frenzied blur of punches to his body and face. He had been so fast before and was able to dodge her attacks easily, but with his foot now held down with her sword, his movement was limited. He couldn't strike back, desperately trying to block her and getting in a swing or two that never landed.

Finally making contact, Voltaris was able to swing his arms around the Oracle and started to put her in a bear hug. Before he could fully embrace her with his thick arms, she raised her hand back, flattened her palm and squeezed her fingers together tightly and jammed the tips of her fingers into one eye. She pulled back and then struck the other eye, shoving her fingers in as deep as she could. He let her go as he reached up towards his eyes and she flipped backward. She jumped back and was standing by his fallen axes. She picked them both up and rushed back at him as he tried to see what was happening. She jumped up and spun one axe sideways while drawing the other up in the air. She came down near his head and the side spinning axe struck first, hitting him across his chest. A moment later the downswing of the second axe landed straight in the center of his skull.

Voltaris' head split cleanly as the axe dug down through his face and neck, finally resting in the center of his chest.

The Oracle threw herself up on his shoulders as he fell and reached down into the hole between his split head and pulled out a chunk of flesh that was glowing a brilliant blue. She landed on the ground and reached up. She held the glowing mass high and grabbed it with both hands, then screamed as she ripped it apart.

The Forta leader's essence, his soul, exploded into bursting streaks of brilliant light, fading slowly like fireworks on the 4th of July. Voltaris' body was hunched over in a heap.

The fight was over.

The battlefield went still. The Oracle looked down, her hair dripping with blood, dirt, and pieces of her enemy. She looked at what was left of Voltaris, then fell to her knees. I could feel her fading. Her wounds were many and I could sense her pain.

She looked up at Grim and then to me.

"Finish this," she said aloud as she fell to the ground.

CHAPTER 19:
ULTIMATE BATTLE

I sent a message to our team. "You heard her. Move to your new battles!"

The silence turned into chaos.

"Move now!" I yelled into their heads.

I turned back and saw the confusion in Windspider and Metallic Squid's faces once they realized they were facing different opponents. Cal hit the Windspider with some rocks he had gathered in rapid succession and Blue flung some water shots at the Firedemon. I jumped into the heads of my team and Bri and the Watergirl were going at it. Bri struck her across a wing and she fell to the ground, but Watergirl quickly recovered.

Blue had the metal enemy completely off guard. It was still looking around for Cal as shots of heavy water balls hit across its face repeatedly.

I jumped back. Andi was keeping even with the demon but Cal was having a hard time. As he threw up an arm, the Windspider blew it past and spun it like an out-of-control boomerang. Once the surprise was gone, it spent its time deflecting.

I updated Kristopher on what was happening.

"We caught them off guard but they're starting to adjust. Any weaknesses on any of them Leo can help with?" I asked.

"Leo found something. He says the Windspider has a soft spot on its outer skin between its neck and shoulder where the wings meet. There are nerve endings where it shoots out energy, but it's a small area, maybe the size of a thumb. He would need to get in close.

I had an idea. I jumped between Blue and Cal.

"Cal," I said in his head. "I'm going to distract the Windspider. We need to catch a shot right in the middle of that indented spot near its shoulder. It's like our human clavicle, I think."

"I broke my clavicle once," Cal thought back to me. "I know exactly where that is."

"We need to keep the wind and energy shots at bay. That's the source of its energy. If you can hit that, it may give us enough time to stop its attack."

"How are you going to distract it?"

I wasn't sure. The wind creature noticed I was staring at it and shot an energy ball at me. Without thinking, I was able to redirect it past me with just my mind. I felt like I was juiced. I hadn't noticed a change in my abilities, but since bonding with the Oracle and Councilman Red everything seemed to be coming easier and this almost involuntary action was a surprise. The sensitivity was increased so much that I was able to feel a threat.

Another shot hurled towards me as its wind power was still spinning with each throw Cal issued.

"Cal, I'm going to try something. Get your limbs back. Let your guard down when I say so and then just imagine you're a pitch away from winning the World Series."

He looked at me and nodded. The Windspider didn't let up, but Cal let his arms boomerang back and land in their sockets.

"Thanks for trusting me," I said. "You may not like what's about to happen next, but it might be worth it."

The Windspider shot out a few quick energy bursts at us.

"You're a hitter now. Lean in and take one for the team," I said to Cal. "Pitcher's about to bean you."

As several energy balls hit Cal, he fell back. The Windspider paused as it saw its shots strike, and that's when I turned the remaining energy around and straight back at it as it focused on Cal.

Getting hit with its own energy shocked the creature and it stared at me then back at Cal, unsure of what happened. I tried to jump in its head but felt the Windspider's confusion and couldn't focus, so I threw in a random burst of energy from behind and to the sides of it and it flipped its head around like it was looking for a fly buzzing in its ear.

"Now, Cal," I said.

Cal stood up and pulled his left arm out of his shoulder socket, straightened it out, then took a full pitcher's stance. He leaned back and went into a short windup. His eyes focused and he had his index finger pointed out as he released his arm. His flying arm was fully extended like a big, pointy javelin. It flew straight and cut through the air.

If there was any doubt this top Texas pitcher had lost his touch it was settled as the arm kept its momentum and Cal's finger struck the Windspider dead center on the soft spot. It came in so fast that it popped as it struck.

The Windspider refocused as its arms reached up to cradle the wound and it fell out of the sky. It tried to shoot out wind and energy but it was like it had lost its breath.

The mouth opened to scream, but no sound came out.

Cal then rushed towards it and shoved his attached hand into the same soft spot as he reached the Windspider and it crumpled. He then pulled his arm loose from the wound and reattached it. Once it popped in, he put his foot down on a wing and pulled on the top of it, ready to rip the wing apart. The Windspider looked up at him and raised its free hand, yielding.

"Leave now and your soul shall be spared," I sent a clear message to the Windspider and Cal now that there was no energy interfering.

The creature looked down. Cal felt its tension ease and let go. The Windspider crawled a few steps and then slowly rose, still unable to gather energy. It floated away from the battlefield and I sensed the moment it was gone.

Blue was at a stalemate and I looked over at Andi and Bri. Bri was gaining some ground on Watergirl. Andi had the demon moving back, but she looked like she wasn't making much headway. Andi shot lines of snot that the demon burned with its fire counter attack as it moved around erratically. I started to run to her to help when my head was filled with her voice.

"Back off! I got this!"

They looked neutral, but she had been slowly getting closer. Each string of snot she shot was still getting deflected. The demon was flying up and back down and I took a look through her eyes.

I realized what she was doing. The demon moved up, then down and swung either left or right before moving a few feet closer, then would repeat and move back. She was studying its pattern and was just trying to get close enough to use it.

On the third pass, the Firedemon was either going to move left or right and that's when Andi made her move.

She had been consistently shooting thin snot streams randomly but this time she took her best guess and shot left with a fat burst of super snot that was oval and messy. The demon cut the same direction, throwing its same small burst to counteract the streams, but it wasn't big enough to handle the large ball she had formed. The snot hit the demon in its face and Andi shot another big one right behind it that hit its ears.

The demon tried to blow fire but the snot that now covered it ears, nostrils and mouth burned a bright orange through the snot. Andi shot more to surround it even further so the fire couldn't escape. The demon's face burned brighter and it shook in desperation, then it just burst. It was like a pimple full of fire and it shot burning snot out of every hole in its face. Its eyes popped and melting pieces of snotty demon body landed all around us. A few pieces hit me. They were hot but our dead bodies were able to withstand it.

The headless part of the demon that was left fell to the ground and blue soul energy floated out.

"Let's go check on the others," Andi said.

She turned back, but I was already in their heads. Blue and Bri were still at a standstill. The few Grunts that Grim and I hadn't destroyed had started attacking them, throwing swords and rocks at Blue and Bri. Bri was able to disappear, but Blue was getting hit. They had moved back several feet from where they started.

Andi ran up between them with Cal and me right behind.

"What do you need?" Andi said as she dodged a flying rock.

"I was making progress," Bri said, "But those Grunts got us back to a stalemate."

Cal jumped in and started taking on the Grunts closest

to him.

I was in all their heads. "Ideas, Blue?"

"Just get rid of those Grunts!" Blue yelled.

I nodded. "I can get us weapons."

I shifted my energy back to the stash of weapons Oracle had refused and sent them our way. Andi grabbed the spiked flail, Cal took several daggers, and I grabbed a spear.

Andi didn't hesitate. She rushed forward after two Grunts threw some rocks and brought the spiked ball down on the top and sides of their heads before they were able to pick up another rock. Cal pulled back the daggers and with his pitching arm nailed three of the Grunts in quick succession.

I tossed my spear without much force but used my mind to give it speed and guide it into the center of one Grunt and I continued driving it through until it pierced through another one behind him. Andi finished off the two last Grunts with her spiked ball.

Now it was just down to the Metallic Squid and Watergirl. Bri quickly gained back an advantage as her fire streams were now closer. As each burning piece neared, Watergirl would send out a wave of water to protect herself and fly off to a side.

"You need something to burn," Andi said as she thought about how she defeated the fire demon. "Be ready to disappear and hit her on my targets."

"What targets?" Bri asked.

"Just watch."

She shot out pancakes of snot that landed like green patches on Watergirl's body. Bri then disappeared and reappeared and fired fast bursts of flame and the snot cakes went up in flames. Watergirl reached at her wounds as Andi shot more pancakes on various parts of Watergirl's body, concentrating heavily on her wings. Watergirl was down but kept flying back up.

"You look like the coolest dragon I've ever seen," Andi yelled.

Dragon. Andi was a genius.

"Bri," I said in their heads. "Become a dragon. All this time we were worried about you staying solid for as long as possible, but use your ability to disappear as an advantage. Make Watergirl think you're ten dragons!"

"I get you," Bri said.

Bri appeared directly in front of Watergirl and the water enemy shot a huge wave at her. Bri popped out and then in rapid succession, reappeared, shot a flame, then popped out and in several more times, faster than I could blink, firing a new wave each time. Watergirl turned but Bri moved so fast she was confused. She turned around after more than ten shots from Bri and seemed to lose her balance in the air.

"Hit her, Andi!" Brianna yelled.

Andi shot a big splat over Watergirl's face and body and Bri appeared directly in front, took in a long snort and let out a wide burning flame at her.

Watergirl fell to the ground, her wings burned and damaged. Bri followed up with another big flame just as Watergirl hit the ground and the blast made her entire body catch fire in one big explosion. The flame burned out and steam sizzled in the air, forming a brief but thick cloud that rose in the air, revealing charred ground underneath. Watergirl was gone.

Bri appeared in front of Andi and hugged her. "Teamwork!"

I took a second to relish the human dragon attack I had just witnessed.

Then I heard Blue. He didn't say anything, but I could sense distress and that his brain was moving but not quite ready to reach out.

"What is it, Blue?"

"I think I know how to defeat it but not sure how I can do it without hurting myself."

"What do you mean?" I said as I moved to him. Cal moved by me.

"The charged metal it shoots. Those pieces hurt when they cut into me but the best way to stop it would be with a big shot of electricity to hopefully overload it."

"So what's the problem?" Cal said.

"I know how to get a source now that you're both here but remember, I'm water."

I realized what he meant. "You'd electrocute yourself, too."

"Exactly. I might be able to stop him but may destroy myself in the process."

"How?" I asked.

"Our secret connection," he thought back.

Of course. He meant the energy of the communication network he had built.

"It can grow stronger than the energy we're using to talk to Kristopher, can't it?" I asked.

I had sensed the potential strength when I was traveling in it but hadn't had a reason to test it beyond what we needed.

"Yes, the strongest signals are when you are communicating. It generates a nice chunk of power."

I got hit with a metal shard in the face. It did hurt.

"I know how to get that power to you," I said, "But not sure how to keep you from getting electrocuted, too."

"I got that," Cal said. "Just do it. Blue, when you hit that thing with water, I'm going to have you stop everything you're doing."

"Are you sure," Blue said, his voice shaking for the first

time.

"You trust me?" Cal asked.

Blue nodded. "I trust you all."

"Do it, Grey," Cal said.

I shot up a message. "Kristopher, I need you to send a constant barrage of words. Don't stop until I tell you. Need to flood our communication line."

"What do you want me to type? I'm not sure what I can do that will go that long."

"Just start reciting the lines from any of our favorite movies."

We had a large library of movies we both loved and sometimes quoted to each other.

"Write out a scene, a line, a song. Just anything."

Kristopher started typing.

"You are a TOY! The force is strong with this one. I'm gonna be a mighty king, so enemies beware."

"You're all over the place," I said.

"Sorry, panicking and thinking about a ton of movies at once."

"That's fine. Just don't stop."

I stayed up in the communication sphere. I sensed something I hadn't sensed before that felt like it was next to me, but down on the battleground. It was behind my view, but I couldn't stop to look now. I gathered the energy coming from the connection with Kristopher and pulled everything I could from the surrounding lines into the connection as he continued to type his movie lines, then jumped back down by Blue.

"It's all gathered up now, Blue," I said. "Tell me when you're ready."

Blue threw a thick stream of water with one hand toward the Metallic Squid but slightly to its side and didn't hit it directly. The Squid moved further aside, thinking it had simply dodged it. With his other hand Blue shot another stream straight up in the air. He balled that hand into a fist and twisted it, making the stream take a sharp turn back down. It then joined the first stream, forming an oddly shaped loop as both streams pressed gently against each other to complete the crooked circle.

More metal shots were coming at Blue and I worked hard to deflect them, taking more hits than expected and each one hurt more than the last. I wanted to flip them back at the Squid, but it wasn't the time.

The Metallic Squid was unfazed with this odd stream Blue was still spinning and just kept shooting different pieces and sizes of electric metal shards, so many that I couldn't deflect them all and some landed on Blue, but he held his concentration and kept it going.

"Fire it down into the stream," Blue said. "Cal, you ready?"

"Do it," Cal said.

I threw my consciousness into the stream as I squeezed my hands together and brought them down in a sweeping motion, guiding all the power from the stream from the upper Underworld atmosphere into a blaze of electric energy and into the stream that was hovering high above us.

The energy came down like a thunderbolt the size of a house and slammed into the wet loop as I jumped back into my body. The water stream electrified and came down in both directions as Blue shifted his arms and moved and widened the stream so that it smothered the Metallic Squid like he was in a gravity-defying waterfall. The electric shock boomed as it made its way down the stream in both directions toward the Squid and Blue. Cal flung both his legs and then as his body fell to the ground, he spun one arm out to follow as he yelled, "Stop!"

Blue clenched his fists and stopped the stream. The Metallic Squid exploded in a flurry of lightning, blinding us all.

Cal's legs landed in the stream just above Blue's head, taking the brunt of the impact that should have hit Blue, immediately followed by his arm that also cracked as the power hit it. Blue flew back when the force hit him dead on as his body was still dripping water.

My ears and head were ringing and we saw bright flashes of light. I looked around.

Blue was sitting up and his hands were shaking and his hair was smoking. Cal was face down with his one arm attached. The Metallic Squid was gone. Andi and Bri had been knocked back but missed the brunt of the force.

"That was your plan?" Blue asked Cal. "Sacrifice yourself?"

"Just my legs and left arm," Cal said. "I figured if I got some body parts between you and the lightning it wouldn't hit you as hard and you'd survive. And as long as it's not my main torso or head, my soul would be safe."

"Why not the right arm?" Blue asked.

"Come on, man. That's my pitching arm. I love you and all, but don't talk crazy."

Andi gathered Cal's charred body parts. They were smoking and burnt, but still intact.

"I think you're going to need the Doctor to fix these crispy things," Andi said as she helped pop them back into place.

The last of our immediate enemies were gone, but that thing I had sensed in the atmosphere now overcame my entire essence. It was behind me. I sensed Grim was down to one last Forta and the Councilmen were still at a stalemate, ignoring all else that was going on.

"Grey," Kristopher's voice popped in. "Almost all

enemy readings are gone. I was about to ask if it was over, but I just picked up something new. A strong energy source. What's going on?"

The disturbance was coming from the Oracle. She was still on the ground, barely moving. Her head was up and she was trying to focus on what I now saw as the source of the disturbance.

A shining gold creature in a robe was hovering over her. A part of the Swarm had moved around it. The rest of the Swarm was still flying above our heads surrounding the Keepers, keeping them from playing any part in the battle so far.

"Kristopher, Oracle destroyed Voltaris and we defeated the others. There's definitely something new here, but I'm not sure what I'm looking at. Keep the channel open."

Whatever the gold-robed thing was floating above the Oracle was psychically strong. Not as strong as the Oracle, but the Oracle was almost completely out of juice right now. I tried to jump into its head.

She was an assassin. It didn't take long for me to get her background as she gave it to me willingly. Everything but her name. Goldie would have to do.

She was a psychic assassin. Voltaris hired her just in case something went wrong and the Oracle survived. Her job was to destroy the Oracle if he couldn't. Apparently he wasn't as confident as he had sounded. She had no business with our Underworld battle and was from another realm outside the Underworld. She was simply there to do her job.

Goldie turned to me and said, "Now you know what I am. Do not intervene."

As she turned back, she tossed me out of her head with a fierce force that left me disoriented.

She was throwing her energy into the Oracle, trying to

break her apart, but even weakened, the Oracle was strong. There was no way she would last long, but it wasn't going to be that simple.

"What's happening?" Andi said.

I sent them and Kristopher a flash of what I knew.

They all started to attack as I tried to get back into Goldie's mind. Grim heard my message and jumped towards us, but the last Forta pulled him back into a fight.

The Golden Assassin waved a hand and my companions were all flung back. Fire, water, body parts and snot were all tossed aside like paper.

I looked around. She was too strong for them. It had to be element versus element. She needed a telekinetic equivalent, and I was the closest thing to it. She was stronger than I was. I knew that immediately, but I also hadn't tested my newly boosted strength.

I moved closer and threw the Swarm aside without much effort. She didn't flinch and continued to throw stronger and stronger mental energy towards the Oracle.

I shot my own energy to her head to try and disrupt it. I hit it gently, and she turned a hand toward me and tried to fling me back as she had done to my friends.

I felt it hit my body and again without thinking, flipped it back. I continued to step.

She turned to face me now. She looked directly at my eyes and threw both hands and a much more powerful burst of energy at me.

This one hit me hard even as I tried to deflect it. I fell on my back but didn't go flying away. I stood back up and kept going. She had already refocused on the Oracle and I saw the Oracle's eyes move toward me and she was able to send out one faint thought.

"I can't anymore, Grey."

The Oracle invited me into her head. She was almost

gone. Her life force was diminishing as the assassin powered up her strength.

I felt the Oracle fading. No. This wasn't going to happen. I loved this Oracle who had been a guide to us all. I loved my Dead Club, I even loved Death himself. The Oracle meant too much to me and my friends. If she was going to die, I was going to die trying to save her.

I felt my eyes gloss over and my fingers tighten as I tried to cup my energy into my palms.

I felt the energy all around me. I felt it above. Kristopher was still typing his movie lines.

I grabbed that energy as hard and fast as I could and then gathered in all the force from every being I could find on the battleground. I blasted it out at her and as I got closer, I threw a fist of energy into her side.

The communication energy came down from Underworld atmosphere and struck us both as I struck her. It hit us at the same time and I blacked out. I was awake a second or so later and my head was pounding, but she was down, too. She looked at me in shock. She crawled a short distance and eased her way onto her feet, never taking her gaze off me.

"I was not aware another possessed the strength you have."

She stood up. I was still seeing stars.

"But it ends now."

She spun her hands in slow circles like she was letting sand pass through her fingers and I felt her energy concentrating. She threw two energy masses at me and the Oracle and the pain was unbearable.

I tried to gather my own energy but was tapped out. I had used all that I could pulling in the atmospheric energy and I was spent. Then the pain overtook me. She kept striking my body and mind and I felt the Oracle fading with me.

"Grey, what's wrong? Hit her back!" Andi said in my head.

"I need mental energy," I said to her. "Something I can pull from. Hurts."

Golden Girl hit us again.

I felt like I wanted to sleep. The pain subsided into something bearable, but I was fighting to keep my eyes open.

"Your mental energy is draining," Goldie said. "It will be gone by the time I'm done. Then this will be over. It matters not whether you win or lose this war, but my mission will be accomplished. I only care to destroy the Oracle, but you will be a bonus."

Then I sensed it. Around me, I felt four strong fields of energy growing. Four familiar sources.

Andi. Blue. Cal. Bri.

They were all honing their power. Blue was gathering up to strike with a water attack, Cal was throwing his arm in a boomerang, catching it and re-throwing, Andi's hands were dripping with wet snot and Bri's hands were glowing with fire, ready to unleash. They were all generating their power without letting them loose, gathering stored energy without releasing.

"Take it," Andi said.

I did.

I pulled that strength and energy they were generating from each of their bodies as they offered it and combined it with what little energy I had. I thought of water and fire and snot and guided it with the accuracy and speed of Cal's arm. My body rose as it enveloped me and then I didn't feel the pain anymore. Goldie was hitting me with everything she had but I felt none of it. I sensed the heat of flame, the stickiness of snot and the wetness of the water throughout my body, emanating as a mix of energy. I pulled them all together and then looked at Goldie. I focused on the center of her chest and suddenly saw the big target. I reached back with both my hands and pulled all the energy into one big mass of blended power and threw it as hard as Cal throwing a fastball. Goldie's energy was at full power but it didn't matter as I hit her with the Dead Club's combined powers. My shot landed clean and when it hit her, she simply disintegrated. There were no pieces or parts or counterstrike. She simply obliterated into nothing.

The energy knocked everyone back. The Councilmen, Grim, the Keepers and the Swarm were all on the ground.

The Oracle wasn't moving.

Grim got up and without hesitation, shoved his bony hands into the body of the last remaining Forta and pulled out his essence.

"You're over," Grim said as he pulled its soul into his mouth and swallowed.

Councilmen Pink and Green then went to their knees as Councilmen Red, Purple and Yellow put their hands on their heads.

"They have conceded," the Spokesman said aloud. "They know they cannot win. It is our way."

We all turned toward the Swarm that had isolated the Keepers and attacked. They held on for a few seconds but with so many different attacks coming at once, they broke apart and flew off.

The Battle for the Underworld was over.

The Oracle remained in the center. She wasn't moving.

I stood over her as Grim reached out and picked her up. We stood around her.

"Is she breathing?" Cal asked.

Grim shook his head. "I don't sense any life. Grey?"

I was already checking her. I sensed no more life force. I slowly shook my head.

"The energy," Blue said. "You were sending that out left and right. Can you give her some?"

That energy had helped bring Andi back and was what Goldie the Assassin was trying to drain from her.

I had spent everything I could on the last strike, but this was the Oracle. She shouldn't need as much.

I looked down as Grim held her. "Grim, set her down, please. Just for a moment."

He eased her on the ground. I put my hands on her head and nodded towards the others.

"Together."

Blue, Andi, Cal and Bri placed their hands gently on her. We had her covered from her head to her feet.

"Gently," I said. "Do what you did for me."

Just as before, they each let out stored energy without releasing anything that would burn her, soak her, stick to her or strike her. Instead of pulling the energy together, I let it surround her body until it covered her in a gentle glow. I expanded the energy and let it ease into her body, like a psychic, electric oil penetrating through her skin. I wanted it to encompass every part of her so she could take whatever she needed.

I sent three more pulses of energy in and closed my eyes, concentrating. I looked in deep until I was sure I was near her soul. I felt a calm sensation. Peace.

I removed my hands. I could feel everyone looking at me as they slowly removed their hands, too.

"Is she..." Grim's voice cracked.

The most sentimental I'd ever heard Grim get was when he spoke of our friendship and his first love. I never figured Death could truly feel, but in that moment I realized he loved her completely. We all did.

I put my hand on Grim's shoulder. I looked him in the eyes and smiled.

The Oracle opened her mouth let out a big breath. Her head turned. Grim placed his hands on her face and he looked back up to me.

"Grey," Kristopher broke in. "I've heard bits and pieces and know the last enemy is gone. What's happening with everyone? Is the Oracle okay?"

I sent up a simple message. "We won. All is well and we couldn't have done this without you. We're still standing and the Oracle will be fine. I can't thank you enough."

Grim started to move his mouth and "Thank..." was all that came out.

"It's okay, Grim," I sent a private mental message to him. "She means the world to us. We love her, too."

The Oracle's eyes opened and she focused on all of us. I felt her relief as she realized she was still with us.

"It's over?" she asked. "The Underworld is ours again?"

Grim nodded. "And I'm forever yours. I want to spend the rest of the Afterlife with you. Marry me."

Tears welled up in her eyes and her smile hardened. "Really. I look horrible and this is when you decide to finally propose?"

Grim looked straight at her. "You look more beautiful at this moment than any other time I have ever looked at you."

Her smile returned. "Grimmy. You know the answer is yes."

She hugged him and then looked each of us in the face. "Thank you all. I told you that you were more powerful than you knew. You just had to prove it to yourselves. You were the difference in this war."

"You are the reason we got here," Andi said. "You were with us the whole time, even when you were almost gone."

"It was all of us," I said. "Everything and everyone that we've been a part of since the day we arrived and everything that has happened since we all came together. All of that combined to save you and the Underworld."

"There's so much to do," the Oracle said as she slowly got to her feet.

"Yeah, this cleanup is not going to be fun," I said.

"No, I mean for the wedding. Brianna, Andi, as soon as I am healed, I'm going to need your help."

It had only been a few minutes since we saved the Underworld. How quickly priorities changed.

CHAPTER 20:
EPILOGUE - A NEW UNDERWORLD

The cleanup from the battle took another three days. The Oracle rested through most of it. Grim wouldn't let her get out of bed and The Doctor was personally assigned to her by order of the Councilmen.

The Council banished the traitors Pink and Green, choosing not to destroy them but to keep them imprisoned. The three remaining members had been convening during the cleanup effort. Things had to change, but none of them were sure how.

The Underworld races, especially the Keepers, helped make the cleanup fast and efficient. There was little evidence of a battle except for the damaged walls and scorched grounds. The Oracle insisted we leave that as-is so no one would ever forget. Leo also wanted it preserved since he wanted to be sure it was accurate for the history books. He was thrilled to leave the library and chronicle events with unprecedented detail. He would never admit it, but he was also excited that he was part of this story. His details on the weaknesses and enemies we faced made for great new volumes and the new aspect of our communication was something new and unique that both he and Blue created.

As a condition of sparing their lives, Councilmen Pink and Green lifted all of the protective measures they had in place. This freed Brianna from her partial existence and she was now fully physical in the Underworld. Although they hadn't targeted her specifically, the enchantments indirectly put her in her previous state.

Once we were done helping, we retreated to our headquarters at the Saloon. We didn't get much time to rest. As we sat there, just our original Dead Club, I looked over at Bri and Cal, holding hands as they spoke.

"Brianna," I said. "There's something I've been wanting to ask you but am a little afraid to."

She stood up and we all looked towards her. "I know the question. You want to know if I'm staying or leaving again."

"That's what I think we were all wondering."

"Yes, Grey. I left before because my Nana said she would be waiting for me and I had to know that she was okay. She was also part of the reason I came back. Now I know she is fine without me and I am needed here. I also missed all of you."

She looked at Cal as she said this and he smiled back. She missed one of us more than the rest, but I didn't mind.

"Besides, I have until the end of time if I want to change my mind, right?"

We all got up to hug her. We all knew we were stronger with her.

A little later that same day Grim appeared. The Council wanted to see us and it was urgent.

We arrived at the Council Chambers. I could sense all the protective enchantments had changed and the same protocols didn't seem to be in place. However, a familiar face greeted us. Morta, the Council Chambers Greeter who we hadn't seen since the Council was first attacked.

"Hello, Morta," I said. "It's good to see you again. I wasn't sure if you had survived."

"I was banished, but the Council restored me. I have healed and was asked to return to my duties," she said, cupping her three-fingered hands together. "Please come with me."

I turned to Grim as we followed. "Is the Oracle going to be here?"

"Yes. We have all been summoned."

The Oracle was standing with the Council when we arrived in the main chamber. She looked great compared to the last time we'd seen her.

She smiled at us as we approached. "Before you ask, I'm fine. This is too important for me to miss and I insisted on being here. Project Wedding will commence soon."

We stopped before the Council. The remaining three members greeted us. Councilman Red spoke first.

"Thank you for coming so quickly. We haven't had a chance to speak since the battle, as our primary duty was to keep our Underworld governance in place."

"So, everything is good then?" I asked.

"Not exactly."

"What's the problem?" Andi asked, ignoring all formalities, although it seemed nothing was formal at this point.

The Spokesman looked to each of us and then to his fellow Councilmen.

"We have spent the last few days without rest, trying to determine the best course of action. The one thing we all agree on is that we cannot keep the same type of Council as before. This incident proved that our Council is not incorruptible. We need a better way and we are not sure how to do it. We have asked you all here to provide some ideas. We have weighed many options, but cannot agree on a method to guarantee this never happens again."

"How about allowing non-Dommerians to serve on the Council?" the Oracle said. "Other Underworlders."

"Yes, that seems to be the most logical decision, but we cannot determine how best to do so."

I had assumed they would just get two new Dommerians but to hear them questioning themselves was oddly comforting.

"The problem is you're looking for a guarantee," I said.

"What do you mean?"

"There is no way you can guarantee that any being won't be corruptible. It seems like a big problem was that many of the decisions the Underworld Council made were done behind closed doors without any additional input."

"Yes, we always know what is best," the Spokesman said without hesitation.

"However, in this case you didn't. There was no way to foresee what was going to happen since you were so confident in your rule," I said.

"That is true," the Spokesman said. "What do you suggest?"

"As the Oracle stated, allowing others to serve is key. I think adding new members who are actually involved in the daily workings of the Underworld is critical. The Oracle and Grim are the most obvious choices. They each have a unique perspective on what's happening and know how things should work and when something is wrong. I think even Leo would make an excellent addition since he knows the history of everything. He is much more than a librarian or historian."

The Councilmen turned to each other and broke into a

loud whispering discussion.

"This does make sense," the Spokesman said. "Oracle and Grim, would you consent to such a role?"

"Would I relinquish my current duties?" Grim asked.

"No, you would simply relegate to your Reapers when Council business arises," he said.

"Can I get some of my restrictions lifted?" Grim asked.

Grim had gone a little overboard in scaring the souls he knew were bad prior to judgment and had been given limitations several centuries before.

"We are open to discussion. The new Council can decide."

"Then I agree," Grim said.

"Oracle, your thoughts on the matter?"

"I would love to have a say," she said. "I haven't always agreed with some of the Underworld policies, and now I can voice that."

Leo then entered the room.

"I was summoned?"

"Leopold von Michelet, the Council is rebuilding and would like to formally offer you a position as a Council Member. You can still keep your historian and librarian duties."

Leo was taken aback. "Me, part of the Council? This is unprecedented!"

"The Council must exist to do what is best for the Underworld and we need to change. You will join Grim and the Oracle, who have already accepted."

"I would consider it an honor," Leo said as he bowed.

"I guess that's been decided, then," Blue said.

"Not quite," the Spokesman said. "Now our numbers are at an even six. With varying opinions, we require a deciding vote, which is why we were always five members."

"Who else are you thinking about?" Cal asked.

"The Dead Club. You have more than proven yourself to be an integral and necessary part of the Underworld. We would ask that your leader Grey become a permanent member of the Council."

"What does that mean, exactly?" I asked.

"You will relinquish your duties as the leader of The Dead Club. Leo, Grim and Oracle have their required duties, but we would require your undivided attention as your duties adjust based on the needs of the Underworld. As there are already four other active members, we feel they can carry on alone."

I turned to my team. They looked at me and then looked down.

I started to shake my head.

"It's okay," Cal said. "They need you. You can represent us all."

"I can't," I said.

Blue and Bri put their hands on my shoulders.

"Grey," Andi said. "You're more powerful than all of us. That's obvious now. You're in a class by yourself and I know you'll do what's best for the Underworld."

I didn't want to abandon my team. I thought about what we needed and the needs of the Underworld as a whole. I knew this was the most important thing. They weren't going to let me say no.

"We must agree to this if we are to get our new government in place," the Spokesman said. "The faster we do this, the sooner we can start governing. We have many decisions to make for those who are still here in the Underworld and what to do with those who tried to betray us."

I looked up. I had to decide now.

I turned back to my friends. "Wouldn't any of you want to do this?"

They all looked at each other but didn't want to reply.

"Of course you would. It's important and we all earned the right."

"Things change," Cal said. "You're going to a bigger team. Plus, maybe now I get to be the leader."

I nodded and turned back to the Council.

"I accept."

The Spokesman smiled. "Please, let us convene and make this official."

Four seats lowered to the ground. Grim, the Oracle and Leo took their seats immediately. I looked back at my friends. I could see and feel the disappointment in them hidden behind the smiles. I knew because I felt it, too. This was happening too fast.

I took my seat and it made a soft humming sound. All four seats rose up to the same level as the Council.

"As the first official act of the new age of the Council, we must vote on ratifying the new members," the Red Spokesman said. "Only the original three may vote. Councilmen Purple and Yellow, I propose that the Oracle, the Grim Reaper, Leopold and Grey Gomez be ratified as full Council members with the power to help make decisions for the good of the Underworld."

"Actually, before we vote, I have something to ask."

"Please, Grey. Proceed."

"The colors. If we are going to be truly united, I think we should all know your true names."

The Councilmen stared at each other.

"This is unheard of," Purple said.

"This entire situation is unheard of," I said.

The Spokesman nodded. "You are correct. We shall start as equals. My true name is Jonique."

"I am Alamke," Yellow said softly.

"I am," Purple said, still struggling. He stopped and

took in a breath. "I am Ikail. I do not remember the last time I spoke my own name."

"Jon, Al and Ike," Cal said. "Y'all fit right in."

"It's good to finally meet you," I said.

"Now, may we return to our vote?" the Spokesman Jonique asked. "The motion is to ratify our new members. I vote yes. My fellow Councilmen Alamke and Ikail, how do you vote?"

They both nodded in approval.

"Then it is by unanimous decision the new Council is ratified," the Spokesman said.

My teammates clapped as they looked on.

I looked down at them and back at my fellow Councilmen.

"I have a proposal," I said as a thought occurred to me.

"Our first proposal as a new Council," the Spokesman said.

"In our democratic Earth government, we have checks and balances. Putting the Oracle, Grim and Leo in the Council helps keep that check in place. As I was chosen to prevent a locked vote, I'd like to propose an additional change."

"What is your proposal?" the Spokesman asked.

"I propose that my seat be vacated," I said.

"Vacated? I do not understand. You were just ratified."

The Council and the Dead Club were all looking at me, confused.

"Vacated and modified," I said. "Rather than keep me as a permanent member, I propose that the original five Dead Club members, which includes me, Brianna Angel, Cal Nolan Griggs, Blue Tipton and Andromeda—"

I heard a loud stomp and knew it was Andi.

"I'm sorry, and Andi Lane, shall represent one position. We have the most unique perspective as we are still pretty new and will be involved in various aspects of the Underworld. As a matter comes up for discussion or a vote, we five will have our own internal discussion that will represent one Dead Club vote to the Council. This adds another layer that won't rest on just one person. As such, rather than having me permanently be here, we can rotate one member when needed so we can stay together. Most importantly, I can remain part of this Club. We function best as a team, with each of us a part of the whole. Removing any one of us, as we already proved with Brianna, weakens us. We are stronger together and can have representation and still exist to fulfill our adjusting duties."

The Council members turned to each other. Grim gave me a thumbs up.

"That makes perfect sense to me," the Oracle said. "They definitely have their own unique perspective none of us here can fully understand."

"The proposal is on the floor," the Spokesman said. "We agree that is an excellent modification. I call a vote."

The original robed Councilmen all nodded.

"I vote yes," the Oracle said.

"I concur," Grim followed.

Leo cleared his throat. "Agreed."

"I say yes," I said.

"The first proposal of the new Council is passed," the Spokesman said. "The Dead Club will hold the seat and may alternate as needed to keep them intact. You were all originally brought here to find out what was wrong with the Underworld. We mistakenly thought that was answered, but now it is obvious that this is a permanent need."

This time my teammates cheered loudly.

"You really didn't want me to be leader, did you?" Cal

asked with a big smile. "Good move, Grey."

"Does that mean I can sit in the chair?" Andi asked. "Looks cool from down here."

After letting each Clubber ride on the chair, we moved to our first discussions on the reformation of the Underworld and how to better our system.

This became known as the first day of the Underworld's Modern Age.

After a long day of discussions, as the first few items came up for a decision, I met with the team to determine our vote. We had all lost our Earthly lives so young, without truly living our lives. It was something I thought about from time to time, but it was on this first day I realized we were given so much more. We were all a part of a larger world that impacted the soul of every living being, including our loved ones back on Earth. We had found a purpose and knew we were making a difference.

As the day ended, we started to leave the Council Chambers to head back to our Headquarters when Grim appeared.

"There is one last item to discuss before you go," he said in a serious tone. "Follow me."

We walked out of the Council Chambers. Our Red Robin was sitting on the outer grounds, waiting to take us back.

Grim raised his hands and the Robin burst into flames, exploding in a fireball that made us all jump back.

"How are we supposed to get back now?" Cal groaned.

Grim clapped his hands together and bright flames shot from his eyes to where the remains of the Robin were smoldering.

There was a metallic groan and a cloud of smoke appeared then slowly faded.

"What is that?" I asked.

"This," Grim said as the smoke dissipated. "Is your new ride. Since your HQ is an Old West Saloon and you've all ridden dead horses before, I figured a fully loaded Mustang GT 5.0 would be appropriate. Convertible, of course."

The car was breathtaking. It was red with black leather on the inside and the front license plate had the letters "TDC" on it. None of us spoke or moved as we let it sink in.

"This is ours?" Andi asked.

"It belongs to the Dead Club. You earned it. Plus now, I won't have to worry about anyone hurting my Cadillac Eldorado."

We forgot how tired we were and jumped in, taking turns driving it. We even let Grim take a spin. It was nice not to have to worry about the weight of the Underworld and just feel the energy of driving our new wheels. We laughed and screamed and loved every moment of it. I would never forget this incredible day.

Life may have taken us early, but even with a name like The Dead Club, we were truly living.

Andi, Blue, Cal, Bri and I became friends on the day we first arrived, but now we were a part of something bigger that went beyond anything we could have ever imagined.

We were family.

ABOUT THE AUTHOR

Manuel Ruiz is a life-long Texan with a passion for reading, video games and music. Since graduating from Texas A&M University Kingsville, he has worked in the IT industry, played in an 80's band, and pursued his love of writing. He published his first novel in 2015, usually writing fantasy with a supernatural twist, and enjoys sharing his love of the arts.

Manuel currently lives in Round Rock with his family where he spends time giving the characters in his head something new and interesting to do.

To find out more, please visit his website:
www.manuelruiz3.com

ALSO AVAILABLE FROM MANUEL RUIZ[3]

The Dead Club
The Dead Club: Councils and Keepers

Lobo Coronado and the Legacy of the Wolf

FREE STORIES!

Subscribe to Manuel's e-mail list to get FREE short stories. Go to his website to sign up!

www.manuelruiz3.com

SOCIAL MEDIA

Facebook:
www.facebook.com/ManuelRuizThree

Twitter:
@ruizman

SPECIAL THANKS

Alpha Readers

David, Mari and Daisy

Beta Readers

David Riskind
Michael Sawyer
Mari Molina
Belynda Chapa
Pam "PMoney" Marino
Daisy Ruiz